"A lap dance with the waiter?"

Cecilia shook her head. "Are you insane? I can barely get the guy to give me a straw with my drink."

Dannie shrugged. "Hey. You picked Dare, and that's the dare. Take it or leave it. But if you leave it, you know what happens."

The Fallback Dare.

"In the case of forfeit of an Official Dare," Cecilia intoned, "the Daree shall be forced to perform the Fallback Dare, which shall consist of phoning her current crush, and confessing all feelings she might have to such crush."

She pictured that phone call in her mind.

Hello, Jake? This is your boss, Cecilia. I think you're really, really sexy, and I want you to know that even though you are my assistant and I'm just about old enough to be your mother, I have smoky sex dreams about you almost every night.

Donna Birdsell

Donna Birdsell lives near Philadelphia, where she absolutely doesn't get any of her ideas from her perfectly normal family, friends and neighbors.

She's addicted to reality television and chocolate, loves a good snowstorm and cooks to relax.

She spent many years writing press releases, newsletters and marketing brochures until a pregnancy complication kept her home from the office. She needed something to keep her busy, so she started her very first novel.

Five years later her dream of becoming a published fiction author came true when *The Painted Rose*, her first historical romance, was released.

She is excited about writing for Harlequin NEXT.

You can reach Donna through her Web site at www.DonnaBirdsell.com.

THE Next NOVEL ™

Donna Birdsell

Madam of the House

MADAM OF THE HOUSE

copyright © 2007 by Donna Birdsell

isbn-13:978-0-373-88136-9

isbn-10:   0-373-88136-3

This is a work of fiction. Names, characters, places and incidents are
either the product of the author's imagination or are used fictitiously,
and any resemblance to actual persons, living or dead, business
establishments, events or locales is entirely coincidental.

This edition published by arrangement with Harlequin Books S.A.

 HARLEQUIN®

PRINTED IN U.S.A.

From the Author

Dear Reader,

I'm an '80s junkie.

What can I say? The music, the fashion, the valley-girl vocabulary. Totally awesome!

I was in high school in the '80s, and the decade brings back fond memories of big hair, big shoulders, big belts and big dates.

It also brings back fond memories of hanging out with my girlfriends, gossiping, doing our nails in study hall, debating who was the cutest boy in Spanish class and which guy from *The Breakfast Club* would probably be the best kisser. (I always voted for Emilio Estevez.)

I got many letters from readers who said the first Truth or Dare book, *Suburban Secrets*, brought back lots of good memories for them, too. I hope this book does the same. I also hope it brings a brief, thoughtful moment about why we, as a society, view older-woman/younger-man relationships with relative disdain.

Most of all, though, I hope it makes you laugh.

Come visit my Web site at www.DonnaBirdsell.com, where you can take an '80s quiz, e-mail me, or share your own memories by posting a message to my blog.

Best wishes,

Donna Birdsell

P.S. Many thanks to Susan Yannessa for her help with the real estate particulars. Of course, any mistakes are purely my own!

For Laina.
You should write a book.

CHAPTER 1

"Kid," Monty had told her, a half-smoked Cuban cigar dangling between his teeth—the permanent accessory accompanied all of Monty's words of wisdom—"the best piece of advice I can give you is this—personal availability is the key to making sales. When you get a call from a potential buyer, drop everything."

Cecilia Katz, known in southeastern Pennsylvania real estate circles as The Madam of the Million-Dollar Deal, had come to realize that everything in life could somehow relate back to the tenets imparted to her by her late mentor, Montgomery Frye.

Monty Frye was a firm believer that real estate equaled life. That if you didn't put your whole heart and soul into a sale, you weren't worth the paper your license was printed on. That if you weren't willing to forsake all else to meet a client for a showing, you may as well be selling time-shares in the Poconos.

So when the muffled strains of "Viva Las Vegas" echoed through the silence of St. John's Episcopal Church, distracting Monty's mourners from one of the most uninspired eulogies Cecilia had ever sat through, she didn't hesitate to answer her cell phone.

She dug through her purse, finding it wedged between a half-eaten PowerBar and an electronic lockbox she needed to put on the door of a house she'd just been contracted to sell.

"This is Cecilia," she whispered into the phone.

The elderly woman beside her gave her an acid look.

"Hang on." Cecilia hunkered into a crouch, working her way to the far end of the pew while, at the pulpit, a puffy-eyed golf buddy extolled the virtues of Monty's tee shot.

She hurried up the side aisle of the church, through the vestibule and out the red, arched front door into a blinding October morning.

"Okay. What's up?" She lit her first cigarette of the day, sucking the smoke deep into her lungs. Her exhale doubled as a sigh of relief.

"Marcia Hagstrom wants to look at the Grove place again." The voice of Jake Eamon, her assistant, cut in and out over the crappy connection.

Jake was manning her phone at Belkin-Frye Real Estate while Cecilia and most of the other agents from the office attended the funeral for her unfortunate mentor, who had dropped dead of a heart attack during negotiations on an eight-bedroom, six-and-a-half-bath estate home on the Main Line.

Cecilia hadn't been shocked at the news, but she had been saddened by it. Monty had been her chaperone into the world of real estate, her adviser, her friend and—when she'd finally hit her stride—her stiffest competition. He was now, of course, stiffer than ever.

Still, she felt absolutely no guilt over the fact that she'd left in the middle of the service to take a call. Monty would have done the same—especially these days, when sales were hard to come by.

"You're kidding me," Cecilia said, dragging on the cigarette. "She wants to look at it *again*?"

"Says she's bringing her husband, but they need to do it right away. Maybe she's really serious this time."

Yeah, thought Cecilia, *and maybe when I get home I'll find George Clooney waiting for me in the bedroom in a tuxedo, with a bottle of Cristal and a dozen roses.*

She crushed out the cigarette beneath the toe of her ridiculously expensive black patent-leather pump. "All right. Let's hope the third time's a charm. Tell them I'll meet them at the house in—" she checked her watch "—twenty-five minutes."

She headed for the Carmona Red Porsche Cayenne her husband had surprised her with two years ago, when times were better. Much better.

Now Ben was gone, and when she looked at the pricey SUV, all she could see were the seventeen payments she still owed.

She slid onto the black leather of the driver's seat and

rested her head on the steering wheel. She wasn't a religious person—she'd pretty much ditched the strict Catholicism she'd been raised on when she married a nonpracticing Jew—but she figured as long as she was this close to a church, it couldn't hurt to pray.

"Dear God," she said into the silence of the car. "It's been fourteen years since my last confession. I have a lot to answer for, I know. And I will, soon. I promise. But right now I need a favor." She took a deep breath. "I really, really need to make this sale. I would appreciate it. And I'll try to keep the sinning to a minimum. Thank you."

She made the sign of the cross, lit another cigarette and pulled out of the lot.

"See you, Monty."

If there was real estate in the afterlife, Monty probably already had his license.

AFTER TWO LAPS through the 8,000-square-foot house and twenty minutes camping out in the master bedroom's walk-in closet, Cecilia still couldn't get a read on Grant Hags-trom. Apparently, neither could his wife.

"So? What do you think, darling?" Marcia linked her arm through her husband's.

Cecilia held her breath.

Grant Hagstrom frowned, the wrinkles on his forehead creating a relief map of the Sierra Nevada Mountains. "It's a little ostentatious for my taste."

This from a man with an electric-pink tie and a diamond pinky ring the size of a Frisbee.

Marcia's surgically altered smile grew painfully tight. "Ms. Katz, may I speak to my husband alone, please?"

"Of course."

Cecilia left them in the closet and went downstairs to the massive kitchen, where miles of sandalwood cabinets had undoubtedly required the clear-cut logging of at least an acre of Peruvian rainforest.

She sighed. The house really *was* ostentatious.

From the kitchen she could see the great room, which featured, as her entry in the Multiple Listing Service touted, "Gorgeous Twin Stone Fireplaces!" at either end, and "Fabulous Exposed Oak Beams!" across the ceiling.

Ostentatious, perhaps. But it was a great place. One of a kind.

The couple who owned the house had thrown some legendary parties, complete with helicopter rides, live elephants, fire eaters and—during one unseasonably warm Christmas—imported snow.

Don Grove was a semiretired music company executive who liked to show his clients a good time. Rumor had it the cops had been called out more than once to break up catfights between warring pop divas.

But the Groves had decided to move permanently to their home in London, and Cecilia had been trying to unload the house for nearly nine months. True, a place like this didn't sell overnight. But she hadn't earned her reputation as a closer by sitting on her high heels.

Last year she'd sold more than forty-two million dollars' worth of prime suburban Philadelphia real estate. She'd been in the Platinum Club at Belkin-Frye five years running. This was her *forte*.

She'd never had this much trouble selling a house before. And she had never *needed* to sell a house more. If the Hagstroms bought this place it would mean a huge commission, with her as both the listing agent and the selling agent. Six percent of three-point-two million dollars. Minus Belkin-Frye's twenty-percent cut of that commission, of course.

She could make up a lot of ground with that chunk of change. She hadn't pulled in a check like that for more than a year. The real estate market had been leveling off, and demand for these types of homes—costly showpieces that required a fortune in upkeep—had dwindled. Unfortunately for her, they were the bulk of her business. She'd become a seller of "exclusive" properties.

She gnawed on a fake fingernail, watching as the Hagstroms emerged onto the flagstone terrace by the pool. Through a set of French doors, she could see Marcia's preternaturally smooth face, the red slash of her mouth forming the suggestion of a frown. Grant's back was toward the window, his bulk shifting beneath his wife's glare. Or what would have been a glare, had recent Botox treatments not made all forms of facial expression temporarily impossible.

"Come on, Marcia. Work it," Cecilia whispered. And then she closed her eyes and prayed again.

Wow. Twice in one day.

God wasn't going to know what to do with herself.

JAKE MET CECILIA at the reception desk, looking like he just stepped off the pages of a Neiman Marcus mailer in a moss-green sport jacket and gold striped tie. With his dark hair and money-green eyes, he drew slavering looks from every female in the office—and a few men, too.

Jake walked Cecilia back to her office. "So?"

Cecilia plunked her bag down on her desk and collapsed into the leather executive chair. "They passed."

Jake shook his head. "I'm sorry."

"Me, too. They're the only ones who've even looked at the place in three months."

Jake came up behind her and kneaded the knots in her shoulders with the strong, gentle touch of one who had worked his way through college as a masseur. "I have faith in you. If you can't sell that house, nobody can."

Cecilia sighed and closed her eyes, ignoring the butter-flies in her stomach that sprang to life whenever Jake touched her. He was her assistant, for crying out loud. Her very young, very impressionable assistant. And she was, if not actually at least technically, still married.

But Jake had a knack for making her feel good.

Beneath his buttoned-down good looks beat the heart of a true flower child. His meditation/yoga/karma kind of attitude infused an air of calm into her hectic life and gave her momentary glimpses of what life might be like if she weren't so driven.

And although his eternal optimism drove her crazy, he made up for it by being so much fun to look at.

Jake ended the massage, letting his hands linger a bit too long on her shoulders. Or was that just her imagination?

Or maybe a little wishful thinking? Her mind whispered.

Oh, boy. She was sinning again, wasn't she?

She raised her eyes heavenward. "Sorry!"

"Sorry for what?" Jake asked.

"Not you. Never mind." She scooted her chair up to her desk and shuffled some papers around. "Any other calls while I was out?"

"I don't know what's on your voice mail, but I only got one. Some woman named Dannie. I left the slip on your desk."

"Dannie?" Cecilia dug through the piles on her desk. It had to be Dannie Peters—now Dannie Treat—her best friend from high school. Or one of them, anyway.

She and Dannie, Grace Poleiski and Roseanna Richardson had all run around together. They'd been inseparable, cutting classes, smoking in the girls' room and doing each others' nails in study hall.

She retrieved the pink message slip and checked the number. Yep, it was her. She picked up the phone and punched in Dannie's number with the eraser end of a pencil.

"Hello?" As it always did, Dannie's familiar voice sucked Cecilia directly back to 1984, when her legs were skinny and her hair was big, and her main concern was whether or not she'd let her current boyfriend get to second at the movies on Friday night.

"Hey, Dannie."

"Cecilia!"

"What's up? I haven't heard from you in while. You doing okay?"

Cecilia heard shrieking in the background, and then Dannie's muffled voice. "Richard Andrew Treat. Get the Tinkertoy out of your sister's nose right now. And don't give me that look." Heavy sigh into the phone. "Sorry. Boys."

"Say no more." Cecilia's own son was pretty mellow, but she remembered how her brothers could have brought a Marine drill sergeant to tears when they were kids. "What's going on?"

"We're having a last-minute girls' night out," Dannie said. "I talked to Roseanna yesterday, and we both agreed we could use a little fun. How about you?"

"Count me in. Where?"

"Philly. A bar in Center City called Caligula. They have an eighties night there that's supposed to be a riot."

"Sounds great. What time?"

"How about eight-thirty? We'll get a jump on the young'uns."

"Remember when our nights out didn't even *start* until eleven?"

"Oh, yeah. I remember."

Cecilia heard an awful screeching noise on the other end, then Dannie yelling, "Richard! Matchbox cars do not belong in the garbage disposal!" Dannie came back on the line, breathless. "Cecilia, I have to run. But I'll see you tonight?"

"Absolutely."

Cecilia placed the phone in the cradle and smiled. It would be great to see her old friends again. Especially Dannie, who'd been going through a rough time lately.

Her husband had died suddenly eight months before, on a business trip off the coast of Mexico, leaving Dannie with four kids under the age of six.

Cecilia sighed. Life hadn't gone the way either of them had imagined it would when they were filling out their M.A.S.H. books and conferring with their Magic 8 Balls in study hall.

CHAPTER 2

*Not every property is a winner. The outside might be mint,
but the inside could look like crap in a blender.*

Monty could have been talking about Ben. Mint on the
outside, crap in a blender on the inside.

It was still strange, though, after four months, to come
home and not see him sitting in sweatpants and a T-shirt
at the computer. He'd be watching a stock ticker scroll
across the bottom of the screen, the blue-gray light illuminating the dark stubble on his chin, Coke cans and junk-
food wrappers littering the floor around him.

There had never been a "Hi, honey. How was your day?"
Or, "You look exhausted. Should I cook dinner?"

Maybe a "Banco de Chile is down two points, but it's
going to rally. I can feel it." Or "I just bought five hundred
shares of Sara Lee at rock bottom."

In reality, Ben's self-proclaimed skill at predicting stock
performance sucked. Big time. Before Cecilia had discovered that, though, he'd managed to lose more than sixty

thousand dollars of their joint savings day-trading on the Internet.

She kicked her shoes off near the door and pressed the button on the answering machine sitting on the hall table.

"Ms. Katz. This is Melvin Weber from the Catalina School again." A dry, clipped male voice emanated from the machine. Cecilia's stomach did a little flip. "I'm calling to remind you that we haven't received payment for this semester. Please let us know when we can expect it."

"Ugh." Cecilia exhaled. She stared at the blinking light on the machine. Seven more messages, most of them undoubtedly similar to the one she just heard.

Unable to listen without some sort of fortification, she shed her jacket, unbuttoned the top button of her blouse and grabbed a bag of M&M's from the pantry.

As she munched on a handful, she leafed through the pile of mail she'd brought in.

Bills.

Visa. American Express. Lord and Taylor. Boxwood Country Club.

She was still paying off charges from a year ago. Most of them were Ben's, but she'd done her share of frivolous spending when she'd believed there would be no end to the cash flow.

She picked up an envelope from Cyber-Trade, ignoring the fact that it wasn't addressed to her. If Ben was going to continue to have his mail sent to the house, it was fair game. She ran a fingernail under the edge and slid the state-ment out.

He'd lost another six thousand dollars? Where was he getting the money? He'd cleaned out their joint accounts long ago.

She picked up the phone and dialed Ben's mother's house. Ben answered on the first ring.

"I just opened your statement from Cyber-Trade by accident."

Silence.

"Where are you getting this kind of money, Ben?"

"Don't worry about it."

"Don't worry about it? I'm sitting here busting my butt, trying to pay off the debts you left me with, and you're losing another six thousand dollars?"

"I had some money in savings at work. I never closed out the account when they laid me off, so they mailed me a check last week."

"Then you should have sent it to me, to pay some bills."

"But I'm going to make a killing, Cece. I have a really hot lead on an IPO—"

"Ben, stop," she said. She rubbed a spot on her forehead that had all the markings of an impending tension headache. "Ever since you lost your job, you've done nothing but sit in front of the computer. I know it's hard to get back out there, but you have to try."

"I'm not ready yet."

"Well, when do you think you'll be ready? We've got bills piled up to the ceiling, and I can't handle them anymore."

"That isn't all my fault, you know. I'm not the one with a closet full of five-hundred-dollar shoes. And you're the one who wanted Brian in that private school. It's costing us a damn fortune."

"You mean it's costing *me* a damn fortune," she snapped. She took a deep breath and lowered her voice. "He's got problems, Ben. He needs help."

"The kid would be fine if you'd just leave him alone. Give him some time."

Ben steadfastly refused to acknowledge the complexity of their son's difficulties. It didn't help that all three developmental pediatricians she'd gone to had given them different diagnoses. One put Brian on the autistic scale. Another called it a language delay. The third said he'd catch up with the other children, eventually.

When Brian was a toddler, Ben had insisted his social issues were merely shyness, his speech difficulties just "a boy thing." But as Brian got older, Ben handled the problems by simply ignoring them.

Cecilia, on the other hand, had always taken an aggressive approach. When the school district refused to provide therapy for him because there was no clear diagnosis of his difficulties she discovered the Catalina School.

It had been a godsend. It was a place where her son could get intensive daily therapy and live with other children who had the same types of problems, and it was close enough to visit every weekend.

Although Brian's first few weeks away had almost killed her, their son had adjusted beautifully to the boarding school and was improving every day.

"Brian is getting a fantastic education at the Catalina School," she said to Ben. "But that kind of individualized attention doesn't come cheap."

"That's what it always comes down to, doesn't it? Money." Ben's tone was bitter.

"In this case, yes. When it can pay for the best education for our son, it does."

"Why is everything about Brian? Ten years it's been all about him. I needed a little attention, too, you know. I could have used some sympathy."

Cecilia squeezed her eyes closed. "I *was* there for you, Ben. I tried to be understanding. I know what you're going through is hard, but you've got to pull it together."

"I don't know what you want me to do."

"I want you to see someone," she said. "A psychologist or a psychiatrist or something. I really think you have an addiction."

"An addiction?"

"Yes, a day-trading addiction. It's like gambling. How much do you have to lose to stop?"

"You're always blowing things out of proportion," he argued.

"You don't think losing almost seventy thousand dollars qualifies as a problem?" She could feel a tiny vein pulsing in her forehead.

"It takes money to make money."

How many times had she heard that? Enough to know that he'd never change his mantra.

She rubbed the vein in her forehead and forced herself to calm down. "Whatever. Just send me some money before you blow it all on your IPO, okay?"

"Great. Thanks for the vote of confidence." The dial tone hummed in her ear.

He'd hung up on her. Again.

She grabbed a glass of wine and walked out on the deck, lighting a cigarette and staring out over the lawn.

The green of the seventh hole of Boxwood Country Club, the golf course her development was built around, winked like an emerald through the trees. In one corner of the yard sat a little patch of hard, brown dirt.

Brian's garden, his project for the past summer.

Unfortunately, he'd planted it in a section of the yard that got about thirteen minutes of mild morning sunlight, and never managed to grow more than a single daffodil and a couple of small, rubbery carrots.

They'd eaten the carrots one night with dinner, and she'd never seen her son so proud.

She smiled. He was allowed to come home for the long Columbus Day weekend, and she had lots of things planned. A trip to the aquarium in Camden, and maybe the Franklin Institute. He loved exploring the giant replica of the human heart there, and putting his hand on the static generator so his hair stood on end.

Someday, she hoped, he'd be living with her again, and they could do fun things all the time, not just on long weekends and during the summer.

She blinked against the stinging behind her eyes— Cecilia Katz *did not cry*—and stubbed her cigarette out in the ashtray she kept on the deck.

At least she had a night out with the girls to look forward to.

The last time they'd gone out, they'd ended up in Atlantic City at three in the morning, playing craps with a busload of senior citizens from the Pleasant Park Rest Home in Jersey City.

One hot roller, an octogenarian named Myra, walked away with a stack of twenty-five-dollar chips as long as her liver-spotted arm. But Cecilia and her friends hadn't been so lucky. They'd cleaned all the change out of the bottoms of their purses, maxed out their debit cards, and had to pay the tolls on the way home with a credit card.

But damn, it had been fun.

She needed another night like that. Desperately.

"Let's face it, Cecilia," she said out loud. "You need a lot of things desperately."

CHAPTER 3

Everyone likes a new house. Everything is shiny and the roof doesn't sag. But the older ones, they're the ones with real character.

Caligula, the club where Cecilia was supposed to meet Dannie and Roseanna, was cool and stylish, boasting faux-marble columns and several seating areas strewn with over-stuffed throw pillows and understuffed young women.

Cecilia scanned the room, but Dannie and Roseanna hadn't yet arrived.

She checked her watch. It was early, and the place wasn't anywhere near capacity yet. The hard-core partyers wouldn't roll in until the next shift. At thirty-nine and three-quarters, Cecilia was well past her partying prime, sent down to the minor leagues along with the other Gen-Xers and the kids with fake IDs.

Cecilia grabbed a table and lit a cigarette, watching the door for her friends. A heart-stoppingly gorgeous waiter in a short little toga and gold-leaf headpiece wandered over to take her order.

"Would you like a drink?"

"How about a club soda with lime for now. I'm waiting for some friends."

"Sure thing." He winked, and her stomach fluttered just a little.

She admired the flex of his calf muscles in the laced up sandals he wore. She imagined Jake would look pretty good in that getup.

Oops. Another impure thought for confession. She was really racking them up.

The DJ made an announcement to kick off Caligula's '80s night, and started with one of Cecilia's favorites, "Superfreak" by Rick James. She watched the door as a group of twenty-something women trickled in, with tiny shirts and tiny waists and tiny rhinestone-studded cell-phone purses hanging from their wrists. They pretended to ignore the group of twenty-something guys hanging by the door who were giving them the once-over.

Dannie and Roseanna came in behind the young women, their heads pressed together, laughing. They made no bones about checking out the guys near the door, and much to Cecilia's satisfaction, they got several appreciative glances in return.

The women located Cecilia and navigated through the growing crowd.

"Hey, chicklet!" Roseanna plunked down into one of the seats and gave Cecilia a peck on the cheek. "How's it going?"

"Eh. How about you?"

"Eh."

"How's work?"

Roseanna, a die-hard music fanatic, was a writer for the local music-scene magazine. She always joked it wasn't so much the poor man's version of *Rolling Stone*, it was the really, really destitute man's version.

"I don't know, Cece. Maybe I'm getting too old for this job."

"Oh, come on. You know more about music than anybody I know."

Roseanna shook her head. "I just can't get into the new stuff, you know? I feel like my parents sometimes. I just want to say, 'What *is* this crap? This isn't music.'"

"Well, sit back and relax, 'cause you're not going to hear any of that crap tonight," Dannie said. "It's all oldies but goodies here."

As if to punctuate Dannie's words, a song by Roseanna's all-time favorite band, the Aching Loins, blasted out over the dance floor. The three women screamed.

The hot waiter materialized with Cecilia's club soda.

"No way, Spartacus. Take that back," Dannie said. "And bring us a round of Gladiators."

In a couple of minutes he returned with a trayful of pretty pink drinks.

Cecilia removed the pineapple wedge and took a sip. "Why do they call this a Gladiator?"

Dannie gave her an evil grin. "Because it's gonna kick your ass."

The Gladiator, did, indeed, live up to its name, and by the second round, the girls were making some noise.

They tore up the dance floor to "Love Shack" by the B52s, "You Spin Me Right Round" by Dead or Alive, and "Head to Toe" by Lisa Lisa, and had returned to the table when Roseanna pointed to someone who'd just come in the door. "Look."

A tall woman in a red silk jacket scanned the crowd. She looked familiar.

"OH. MY. GOD. It's Grace Poleiski," Dannie said.

"I saw her at Beruglia's when I went there for lunch today," Roseanna said, grinning. "I didn't think you guys would mind if I invited her."

"Are you kidding!" Cecilia laughed. "It's gonna be just like old times."

AFTER THE USUAL NICETIES about who'd lost weight (Cecilia and Roseanna), who'd lost a husband (Grace, Cecilia and Dannie) and who'd lost the ability to party all night and still function in the morning (all of them), the waiter appeared with a tray of pale-orange shots.

He set one in front of each of them, pulled a pack of matches out of the folds of his toga and lit the shots. Low blue flames danced on the surface of the liquor.

"Don't forget to blow 'em out before you drink 'em," he said. "We've had a couple of mishaps."

Roseanna smiled. "Remember when Dannie accidentally lit her hair on fire while she was smoking a cigarette in the girls' bathroom?"

"What did she expect?" said Cecilia. "She used so much hairspray, her hair wouldn't have moved in a hurricane."

"Come on." Dannie laughed. "My hair wasn't any worse than anyone else's. In fact, I remember Grace getting hers tangled in the volleyball net in gym class. That hairdo had to be at least a foot high."

They all cracked up.

The waiter walked away, his tight little butt all but peeking out from under the toga.

Dannie propped her chin up on her hand. "Those look like my sheets he's wearing."

"You wish," Cecilia said.

Grace pulled a bunch of pictures out of her purse and passed them around.

"Oh, God. I remember this skirt," Roseanna said. "I couldn't get one thigh in there, now."

"Sure you could," Dannie said. "It would be a little tight, though."

"Ha, ha." Roseanna passed the pictures to Cecilia. "Hey, remember when we used to play Truth or Dare in study hall?"

"Yeah. I think Mr. Montrose almost had a heart attack,"

said Cecilia. "You'd always dare me to lean over his desk to ask him a question."

"He couldn't stand up for the rest of the class," Dannie said.

"In his defense, you did have some pretty nice boobs," said Roseanna.

"To Mr. Montrose." Grace raised the shot the waiter had just delivered. They all toasted Mr. Montrose and blew out their Flaming Togas.

"Let's play," said Roseanna.

"Play what?"

"Truth or Dare."

"Here?" Grace said. "You're crazy."

"It'll be fun," said Dannie.

"Why not?" said Cecilia.

Music thumped in the background. Motley Crüe belted out, "Girls, Girls, Girls."

"What the hell," Grace said.

"Who's going first?" Dannie asked.

"I will." Cecilia had been first in lots of things. She'd been the first to get a bra, the first to get her period, and the first to wear gauchos to school.

She was the first girl on the debate team (she never lost a debate), the first freshman to go to the senior prom (with Kyle Farber, the captain of the debate team), and the first one to let a boy see her underwear (Kyle Farber, the night of the prom).

So it only followed that she'd go first. At least, this was the logic after three Gladiators and a Flaming Toga.

"Okay, Truth or Dare?" Grace said.

"Dare," said Cecilia.

Dannie rubbed her hands together. "Great. Here's one. Get our waiter to bring us a round of shots on the house. By whatever means possible."

"Nah, that's too easy," Grace interrupted. "How about she has to get the waiter's phone number?"

"Oh, that's good." Dannie laughed.

"Are you kidding me? Shots? Phone numbers? That's lame." Roseanna closed one eye and tipped her glass toward Cecilia. "Here's a *dare*. You have to get the waiter to give you…a lap dance."

The three other women hooted and clinked glasses.

"A lap dance?" Cecilia shook her head. "Are you insane? I can't get that guy to give me a lap dance. I can barely get him to give me a straw with my drink."

Roseanna snickered.

Dannie shrugged. "Hey. You picked Dare, and that's the dare. Take it or leave it. But if you leave it, you know what happens."

The Alternate Dare.

"In the case of forfeit of an Official Dare," Cecilia intoned, "the daree shall be forced to perform the Alternate Dare, which shall consist of phoning her current crush, and confessing all feelings she might have for such crush."

Cecilia imagined how that phone conversation might go:

"Hello, Jake? This is your boss, Cecilia. I'm calling to tell you I think you're really, really sexy. You smell great, and I love the dimples on your earlobes. I want you to know that even though you are my assistant and I'm just about old enough to be your mother, I have smoky sex dreams about you almost every night."

A wave of queasiness washed over her.

"No copping out," Roseanna warned. "We swore on our posters of Jon Bon Jovi."

"I remember. Jeez. Did I say I wasn't going to do the dare? I never said I wasn't going to do the dare." Cecilia sucked down the rest of her drink and ran her fingers through her hair. "Just…get him over here."

Dannie waved to the waiter, who stood near the drink station at the bar, as still as a Roman statue and twice as gorgeous.

Cecilia's heart sped up to Moderately Dangerous on the heart attack scale. As the waiter neared, he morphed for a moment into Jake.

Cecilia blinked and Jake was gone, but the stud-boy who now stood before her was only a slightly less fantasy-inducing alternative.

She forced herself to stay cool. "Hey, Spartacus, how about a lap dance?"

Grace spewed a mouthful of Gladiator all over the table.

Dannie covered her face with her hands. Only Roseanna was able to keep a straight face.

The waiter's eyes grew wide. Cute. Like Bambi.

Oh, dear Lord. She was propositioning Bambi.

She quickly banished that image from her mind.

"Pardon me?" The waiter said, apparently believing he'd misunderstood.

If only.

"May I have a lap dance, please?" Cecilia waved two twenty dollar bills in front of him, which he pretty much ignored.

"I'm sorry, ma'am, but this isn't that kind of establishment."

She ignored the *ma'am* thing. "What kind of establishment is that?"

"The management doesn't allow hands-on entertainment, if you know what I mean. We have strict rules."

She fished another twenty out of her wallet and added it to the others, fanning herself with the bills. "It wouldn't exactly be *hands*-on, now would it?"

Spartacus had finally taken notice of the bills, and moved a little closer. Close enough for her to smell the fabric softener on his toga.

She fished another twenty—her last one—out of her wallet. There went her lunch money for the next two weeks. She was quite fond of lunch. This lap dance had so better be worth it.

"And if there were no *hands* involved," she continued,

"you wouldn't exactly be breaking the rules, would you?" she said.

"No, I suppose I wouldn't." He glanced around, presumably to make sure no management was watching.

Prince's "Little Red Corvette" blared over the sound system. *Perfect.*

Cecilia drove it home. "What do you say, Spartacus?" She waved the eighty dollars in front of him.

The waiter took the money and tucked it into the folds of his toga. "I say, get ready for the best lap dance you ever had."

"TONIGHT'S GOING TO go down in history as the best Truth or Dare game ever," Dannie said, rubbing an ice cube on her neck.

"It is, isn't it?"

Cecilia puffed on a cigarette, making tiny smoke rings by tapping on her cheek. She glanced over her shoulder at Grace, who sat at the bar sucking face with an unbelievably hot stranger.

They'd dared her to give him the undies she was wearing. And now, it seemed, she might end up giving him a whole lot more.

"I don't believe it," Dannie said. "Look at her. She actually did it."

"She always had guts."

"She sure did." Dannie's eyes held a faraway look.

Cecilia had always been a teeny bit jealous of Grace's in-your-face audacity. Cecilia may have been first at lots of things, but Grace was the group's official rebel. The one time Cecilia had been a rebel herself, she'd gotten nailed for smoking in the dorms at cheerleading camp.

She and her roommate had caused the whole squad to get kicked out of camp, and they had to spend the entire football season on the sidelines, freezing their butts off in those short little skirts.

She exhaled a cloud of smoke. She *really* had to quit smoking. She'd promised Brian months ago that she'd stop by the time he came home for Columbus Day weekend.

She checked her watch. Midnight. Time was officially up.

"Okay, we've lost Grace," Dannie said. "And Roseanna's no good anymore."

Roseanna's head currently lay on the table, on a pillow of cocktail napkins.

"Doesn't matter," Cecilia said. "You're the only one who hasn't had a turn at the game, and I can handle it. Truth or Dare?"

Dannie slumped in her chair. "I dunno. You pick for me."

Cecilia chewed on her straw for a minute. "Okay. Truth. I want to know what's going on with you."

"What do you mean?"

Cecilia leaned in. "I know you, Dannie. Something's wrong. Are you missing Roger?"

Dannie snorted. "Yeah. I don't know what I miss more,

the lying or the cheating." She shook her head. "Oh, God. I'm sorry. I know I shouldn't speak ill of the dead, but he was such a shit." She began to cry.

Cecilia lifted Roseanna's head and retrieved a cocktail napkin, which she handed to Dannie. "He cheated on you?"

Dannie nodded. "At least once that I know of. But probably way more than that." She sighed. "He was a good father, though."

That was Dannie. Always looking at the shiny side of the penny.

"I'm so sorry," Cecilia said. "But you know you could have talked to me about it. Anytime."

"I guess I was embarrassed, which is just silly. Life would be so much better if we could all just share our secrets and get them off our chests. Don't you think?"

"Hmm." Cecilia chewed on an ice cube. "As a matter of fact…"

Dannie dabbed her eyes with the now-soggy napkin. "What? You have a secret, too?"

Cecilia pushed her shot away. "I really have to sober up."

Dannie squeezed her hand. "Come on. I'm your friend. Maybe I can help."

"Well, the thing is, I'm—" Cecilia sighed "—well, I'm flat broke."

CHAPTER 4

Everything is negotiable.

As soon as she said it, she regretted it.

Here she was, complaining to Dannie of all people. Dannie, a widow with four kids, who never had enough of anything.

"Cece, let me help you," Dannie said. "I can lend you some money."

Cecilia shook her head. "No, I'm going to get out of this somehow." She didn't want to tell Dannie that whatever she could lend her wouldn't pay the charge-card bill for Ben's golf shirts.

Dannie looked as if she were going to say something, but stopped.

Cecilia sighed. She supposed getting everything off her chest couldn't hurt. It was a night for truths as well as dares, wasn't it? "The truth is, Ben never even tried to find a job after he was laid off. He started day-trading instead. In the beginning he made some money, but mostly he's been losing. A fortune. My fortune."

"But your job…" Dannie said.

Cecilia shook her head. "The real estate market is tanking. I can't sell a house to save my life. If this keeps up, I'm going to have to start doing open houses again." She felt the dreaded sting behind her eyes again.

Dannie gave her a sympathetic look. "Anything I can do, let me know. Okay?"

Cecilia nodded. She sucked down a glass of water and chewed on the ice as she and Dannie sat there together, lost in their own thoughts.

The first few notes of Bob Seger's "Old Time Rock and Roll" blared over the speaker system. Tom Cruise slid through Cecilia's mind in his underwear, and she smiled. "Oh, screw it. Let's just have a good time."

She and Dannie sang along with the song and reminisced about the night they'd sneaked into a movie theater to see *Risky Business*. They'd only been fourteen, not legally allowed into an R-rated flick, but a friend who worked at the Cineplex let them in.

Years later, Cecilia realized that most of the movie had gone right over her head, but the image of Tom Cruise in his tighty whities had certainly stuck.

"Hey, I know," Dannie yelled over the music. "You could do what Joel did in *Risky Business*."

"What? Hire a hooker?"

Dannie laughed. "No. You know, have a party. Round up some call girls and show some rich boys a good time."

"Right." Cecilia laughed, trying to picture herself arranging a "good time" for her friends' teenage sons. Yuck.

Roseanna raised her head. "Party?"

Cecilia stubbed out her cigarette. "Yeah, there's a kegger out on Creek Road. Wanna go?"

Dannie laughed at the mention of their favorite high school hangout. "Come on. Let's get Rosie out of here."

"Okay, just let me check on Grace first."

Cecilia pushed her way through the crowd to the other side of the bar, where Grace was still sucking face with the leather-clad hottie.

"You okay?" she asked.

Grace nodded.

"How are you getting home?"

"I'll call a cab."

"Okay." Cecilia winked at the guy. "Nice to meet you."

"Likewise," he said. Rose Frost lipstick smeared his lips.

Cecilia felt a flash of envy for her friend. She still remembered that feeling—that out-of-body high—that always accompanied brand-new kisses.

Cecilia returned to the table and waved to Grace. She made a fist and held it to her cheek like a telephone receiver, mouthing the words, "Call me."

Then she and Dannie slung their arms around Roseanna and dragged her through the crowd toward the door.

"Come on, gorgeous. Let's try to get you home before you lose your cookies."

A DULL PAIN throbbed behind Cecilia's eyes as she brewed a pot of coffee the following morning. Her breath smelled like a burned-out distillery, and her fingertips were yellow from nicotine.

She had to stop drinking. She *had* to stop smoking. Today. *Now.*

She took the pack of cigarettes from her handbag and emptied them into the sink, firing up the garbage disposal. The sound bore into her brain like a jackhammer.

Oh, man. This might not be the best day to quit smoking.

Her malaise eased a bit when she realized that in just a few hours she'd be on her way to pick up Brian at the Catalina School.

She hummed "Old Time Rock and Roll" as she flipped through a shoe catalog, planning her afternoon with her son until an annoying beeping sound coming from the street disturbed her thoughts.

It sounded like a trash truck, but it wasn't trash day.

Coffee mug in hand, she wandered through the dining room and into the formal living room, to the bowed window overlooking the driveway. A green-and-yellow truck was backing into the drive. Sunlight glinted off the shiny silver flat bed, which seemed to be falling off the truck.

No, it wasn't falling. It was *tilting.*

She squinted, unable to see too clearly without her contact lenses. What…?

"Shit!" She bolted for the front door, spilling coffee down the front of her robe and onto the white wool carpet.

She reached the steps that led down to the drive just as a large man with an obscene amount of butt-crack showing hooked the rear axle of her Cayenne to a winch.

"Hey!" she shouted. "What are you doing?"

He stood up. "What does it look like I'm doing?"

"It looks like you're trying to steal my car."

He guffawed. "That's a good one."

"No, really. *What* are you doing?"

The guy grinned. "I'm repossessing your vehicle."

"What!"

"Look." He waddled over and handed her a clipboard with a blue form containing her name and address, a description of the Cayenne, the VIN number and the license plate number.

"I don't understand," she said.

He spit a stream of tobacco juice onto the lawn. "You ain't made your payments, lady. I'm taking the car."

"Oh, no. No no no." She read the name in the blue oval above his shirt pocket. "*Ed*, you can't take my car. I need my car."

"Sorry. I guess you shoulda thought about that when you weren't writing those checks." He walked to the back of the truck and threw a lever. The Cayenne slowly began to move up onto the tilted flatbed.

"Stop! You're not listening to me. I—"

Oh, God. What was she going to do?

"I have an emergency. I'm supposed to donate a kidney this afternoon."

Ed snorted. "Like I haven't heard *that* one before."

"I'm delivering toys for underprivileged children?"

Ed shook his head.

She exhaled through pursed lips. "Hang on, please. Wait here one minute."

She ran into the house and found her purse, digging out her wallet. Damn it! Empty!

She'd given that waiter every penny she had for the lap dance.

She ran for the door, stopping briefly at the hall mirror to smooth down her sleep-rumpled hair. Discarding her coffee-stained robe, she ran back outside in nothing but her baby doll pajamas.

Ed's eyes bugged.

"Listen," she said, "I'm begging you. You can't take my car."

Ed's eyes gravitated to her chest, as if they were magnets and her breasts were little refrigerators.

"If I had any money I'd give it to you, I swear. But I spent it all on a lap dance last night."

She could see Ed working the image through his head, and she realized it was probably a much different scenario than the one that had actually occurred.

She wasn't about to bust his bubble.

Tiny beads of sweat formed on Ed's upper lip. He shook his head. "I can't. I have a repo contract with the bank."

"It was a great lap dance," she said, pooching out her lower lip and thrusting a hip toward him.

"Lady—"

"Please, Ed." She reached out and touched the collar of his blue work shirt lightly. Beseechingly. "I'm having a really, *really* bad week."

Dear God, I'll see you in confession on Sunday. I swear. Until then, just one more little favor?

Ed's face softened. Was it possible he'd been influenced by the Supreme Being? Or was he just hypnotized by her breasts?

"I promise I'll take care of this next week," she said in a whispery voice.

Ed shook his head, but ripped the work order off the clipboard. "I guess I could misplace the paperwork for a little while. But if the bank doesn't cancel the order, I'll be back."

"Of course. Oh, wow. Thank you so much."

"Right."

He bent down to unhook the winch, giving Cecilia an eyeful of that special cleavage only overweight service men seemed to possess.

That reminded her. She had a rump roast in the freezer she wanted to thaw.

CECILIA SQUEEZED ONTO a bench in the sauna at the Boxwood Country Club Fitness Center, hoping to sweat out the remnants of alcohol and nicotine from the night before.

The place was filled to busting with women attempting to fight the ravages of age by any means possible. Physical, chemical, surgical—anything to stave off the dreaded sags and bags of middle age.

She stretched out her legs, exhausted from almost an hour on the treadmill, which reminded her of her life right now. Lots of effort to get absolutely nowhere.

The door to the sauna opened and an aerobicized woman with short, bottle-blond hair entered, wrapped in one of the blue-and-white-striped club towels.

"Hey, Marjorie."

Marjorie Almswhite, one of the wealthier women who frequented the club, was a widow with a wicked sense of humor and an eye for young men.

"Hey, Cecilia. Were you spinning?"

"No, just the treadmill today."

"Too bad. Kevin was teaching the spinning class."

The heat seemed to go up a few degrees in the sauna, as all the women audibly sighed.

Kevin Trawler, one of the fitness instructors at the club, wasn't what you'd call classically handsome. But he had a certain naive charm and the tightest butt Cecilia had ever seen. He was also about half the age of most of the women who frequented his classes.

"I know," Cecilia said. "I couldn't get in. The class was filled."

"Early bird gets the worm," said Gretchen Stevens in a smug, singsong voice.

"Are you?" Marjorie asked.

"Am I what?"

"Getting the worm?"

They all laughed.

"As a matter of fact," Gretchen said defensively, "I caught Kevin looking at my boobs today during class."

"Really?" said Marjorie. "Are you sure he wasn't looking at your belly button? They're in the same general area these days."

Gretchen pulled her towel tight around her and huffed out of the sauna, slamming the door behind her.

Some of the women snickered.

Cecilia shook her head. "Getting the worm…"

Marjorie sighed. "Honey, it's been so long since I got a worm like that, I wouldn't remember what to do with it."

"I wouldn't even know where to *get* a worm like that," said Betsy Gardner, the club's resident airhead.

"At the bait shop," Marjorie returned.

"Don't you mean the jail-bait shop?" said Cecilia.

"What? You don't approve?" Marjorie said.

Cecilia shrugged. "Far be it from me to ruin your fishing fantasies. I just think I'd prefer someone a little more… mature."

Liar, liar, pants on fire, her mind whispered, as the memory of Jake Eamon's hands on her shoulders pulsed like a subliminal message through her brain.

She shifted uncomfortably. It was getting *way* too hot in that sauna.

"Who wants an old worm when you can have a nice young one?" Marjorie said.

Betsy leaned back against the wall and closed her eyes. "I hate to break it to you Marjie, but the only way you're getting a nice young one is if you pay for it."

Marjorie shrugged. "Hey, if I knew of a good bait shop around here, I'd shell out in a second."

By the silence in the sauna, Cecilia suspected they were all thinking the same thing.

Too bad it wasn't that easy.

"Let's face it," Betsy said gloomily. "None of us is going fishing anytime soon."

CECILIA MADE a quick stop at the Shop 'n Bag on her way to the turnpike. She'd run out of a couple of things, including ibuprofen, which she desperately needed at the moment, both for her hangover and a raging case of cramps. She also wanted to pick up some of Brian's favorite snacks for the car ride.

She trudged through the store, studiously avoiding the customer service counter and the cigarettes, loading her basket with over-the-counter products she hoped would stave off the symptoms of various ailments she'd been cultivating. Tension headaches from work. Corns from the absurd high heels she'd become addicted to. Pulled muscles from the gym. Heartburn from Ben.

She picked up a bag of salted pumpkin seeds and some granola bars for Brian, and snagged a giant bag of M&M's for herself. Chocolate had powerful healing properties.

At the checkout, she plunked her basket on the conveyor belt and dug through her purse for her VIP card. She held it out to the checker, a young, all-American-type guy with a mop of blond hair, who completely failed to notice she was there.

That never would have happened five years ago.

Okay, *maybe* it would have happened five years ago. But definitely *not* ten years ago.

"So what're you gonna do?" said the checker to the bagger, another frat-boy type. Both wore Temple University sweatshirts.

"I don't know," said the bagger. "I can just about afford beer with what I make here. Tuition? Forget it. I'm going to have to take next semester off."

"Excuse me…" Cecilia waved her card at the checker.

Ignored again.

"But you're supposed to graduate in May, dude," the checker said.

The bagger shrugged. "What can I do? I already have so many loans out, I'm gonna be freakin' forty by the time I pay them off."

"Hey!" Cecilia said.

The boys finally looked at her.

"Forty isn't that old."

The checker's ears turned red. "Sorry, ma'am."

"'Ma'am,'" she muttered under her breath.

The checker unloaded the stuff from her basket and ran it over the scanner.

"Gimme those," she said, grabbing the M&M's out of the bagger's hand and opening them with her teeth.

"Yes, ma'am."

"Stop calling me ma'am."

"Yes, ma—" He clammed up.

The checker scanned the box of tampons she'd picked up, and a knowing look passed between the two guys.

She pointed at the bagger. "Oh, you think I'm just a hormonal old lady, huh? I'll have you know, we old ladies work hard to maintain ourselves. Do you know how many pints of Ben & Jerry's I've passed up for my butt's sake? Do you know how many miles I've logged on the treadmill?"

The bagger shook his head. "No, uh…miss?"

She gave them both a scathing look. "You owe me for that hard work. You, and every other man on the planet. So you better not ever call anyone under eighty 'ma'am' again."

"Yes, miss."

"And one more thing." They looked at her the way men should always look at women—both fearful and expectant. She leaned in. "You better have the decency to watch my ass when I'm walking away."

CHAPTER 5

Whatever you do, don't let yourself get backed into a corner.

In the half hour it took to reach the top of the winding hill leading up to the Catalina School, Cecilia had eaten half the bag of M&M's, added up everything and everyone she owed in her head and chewed her thumbnail down to a bloody nub.

She found a parking spot in the circle outside the boys' dorm and climbed the wide, stone steps to the door, admiring as she did every weekend the placid beauty of the place. No wonder Brian loved it here.

The dorm rested on the crest of the hill, which overlooked a sprawling formal garden arranged on tiers, meticulously maintained since the school opened in the late nineteenth century.

The dorm was swarming with excited parents picking up their kids for the weekend. Most families lived too far away for the weekly visits Cecilia was able to make, so the activity was unusual.

When Cecilia checked in at the desk, a tall, brittle-looking man she didn't recognize greeted her.

"You are here to pick up…?"

"Brian Katz. Room 101."

"Ah, yes. Mrs. Katz."

She didn't care for his tone.

"I'm Victor Newhouse, the new director of student living."

"A pleasure," she said, even though it definitely wasn't. "May I go up to Brian's room?"

"Just a moment, please. Wait right here."

He disappeared into the office behind the desk, and closed the door.

Cecilia leaned up against the desk and watched the bustling in the lobby for a while. She checked her watch. Six minutes.

"Hello?" She called.

Victor emerged from the back room. "Sorry. I had to make a call."

"I see. May I go get my son now?"

"In just a moment."

"I'm sorry. I don't understand. Is something wrong? Is Brian okay?"

"Of course, of course. We…"

The dorm door pushed open, and suddenly it was clear what she'd been waiting for. Or rather, who.

Melvin Weber, the school's finance director, hurried in, his thin blond comb-over flapping up in the gust created by the door's closing.

Cecilia steeled herself.

"Mrs. Katz, I'm so glad I caught you."

That was exactly how she felt. Caught. Trapped. By the look on Melvin's face, he was moving in for the kill, and she couldn't even chew her leg off to get away.

"Mr. Weber, how nice to see you again," she said, shifting into full bitch-queen mode. If she couldn't get away, maybe she could bully him into submission. "I've come to pick up Brian, and I'm in rather a hurry. If you'll excuse me—"

"I'm sorry, Mrs. Katz. But I can't let you go until we discuss your outstanding financial obligation to the Catalina School."

"Outstanding…? I'm afraid I don't know to what you are referring." She did her best imitation of her fourth-grade teacher Mrs. Wickett, who was largely regarded as the meanest teacher in the state of Pennsylvania and was rumored to have been created from a block of ice.

The Mrs. Wickett thing was ineffective in the face of Melvin Weber's crusade.

The finance director patted his comb-over back into place. "Brian's fall tuition, Mrs. Katz. We've attempted to contact you on numerous occasions. Your check bounced."

Cecilia's stomach dropped. Her gaze slid sideways to Victor Newhouse, who looked as if he were wishing for a bucket of popcorn and a box of Junior Mints to go with the show.

"Mr. Newhouse, would you kindly excuse us?" she said.

Newhouse looked at Weber, and Weber nodded. Newhouse looked crestfallen. "Of course. I'll just wait in the office."

"Perhaps you'd be so kind as to go get my son for me, so we can be on our way without further delay."

He hesitated.

"Are you holding my son *hostage*, Mr. Newhouse? Is that what you're doing?"

"Certainly not!"

"Then, will you please go get him?"

Weber nodded to Newhouse.

"Sure. Of course." Newhouse came around the desk and headed up the hall, dragging his feet, clearly hoping to hear the end of the conversation.

Cecilia brushed an errant curl from her forehead. "Mr. Weber, if payment hasn't reached you, I do apologize. We've been having a bit of trouble with our bank accounts, a snafu with account numbers or something, and I asked my husband to handle this matter. However, as you might know, we are estranged, and it's a bit of a messy situation. I assure you that I will send another check first thing on Tuesday."

Weber's lips formed a tight line. "See that you do, Mrs. Katz. I know how much effort you put into getting your son admitted to the Catalina School. It would be a shame if we had to release him."

AN HOUR LATER, with Brian listening to his MP3 player and munching pumpkin seeds in the back of the Cayenne,

Cecilia ate the remainder of the M&M's and chewed the rest of her fingernails down to bloody stumps.

What in the hell was she going to do?

This was definitely *not* the weekend to quit smoking.

She glanced at her son in the rearview mirror. He looked more relaxed, happier, than she'd seen him in a long time.

She simply could not take him out of Catalina.

But where was she going to get the tuition money? She'd been playing musical payments with all of her bills since March, trying to make her commission checks stretch farther than her Aunt Theresa's girdles.

The money just wasn't there.

Her mind flooded with thoughts of torturing Ben. Nothing too severe. Maybe just extracting one of his kidneys with a rusty lawnmower blade. As a bonus she might be able to sell it on eBay.

She counted to ten and cleared her mind. She'd handled tougher situations. There had to be a way to come up with some quick cash.

She'd already taken two ten-thousand-dollar advances on her commission from Belkin-Frye. She couldn't ask for any more, especially now that Monty was gone.

She'd sold off all the antiques in the house that were worth anything months ago, so that was a dead end. She'd gotten advances on her credit cards and a second mortgage on their home, going into more debt to pay debt.

She'd cashed in the retirement account from her first

job, selling pharmaceuticals for a big New Jersey drug company. The penalties had killed her, and she'd lost her matching funds, but she'd been desperate.

"Mom, can we get a puppy?" Brian called to her from the back seat. "Ethan has a puppy."

She smiled. "Not right now, buddy. Puppies are a big responsibility. They take a lot of time." And a lot of money.

She glanced at Brian in the rearview. He was frowning. "But Ethan has a puppy."

"I'm sorry, Brian. But we just can't do it right now."

"But Ethan has a puppy."

"Yes. Ethan's mother is home all the time."

"Why aren't you home all the time?"

"Because I work, honey. You know that."

"You work a lot."

"Not enough these days," she said, mostly to herself. She sighed. "If we got a puppy, wouldn't you like to be here with it? Maybe we'll get one when you come home for the summer."

He stared out the window.

Brian wasn't good with waiting. Didn't understand the concept, really. To him, anything that wasn't happening in the present wasn't happening at all. When he was younger, he used to throw the most awful tantrums, screaming and thrashing when he couldn't have something the minute he wanted it.

Ben, and many of their family members, had seen it as

Brian having been spoiled. But Cecilia suspected it was something different.

It was as if her son had no concept of time. He didn't understand "soon" or "tomorrow" or "later," or any of the other words that could give him hope. If he wanted a toy or a book or a snack, these words meant nothing. While other children heard promise in these words, Brian only seemed confused and dejected by them.

In the back seat, Brian started rocking.

Cecilia resisted the urge to drive straight to the pet store. A puppy wouldn't fix this. Wouldn't fix *him*.

Experience told her that Brian would soon move on to something else, and that his disappointments would be many, over the weekend. But thankfully none of them would last too long.

A few minutes later he said, "Did you know there are 512 M&M's in a one-pound bag?"

"But this is...*was*...a two-pound bag," she said. "How many were in this one?"

Brian looked out the window for a moment, and said, "One thousand and twenty-four."

She smiled and said, "Very good, honey!"

Meanwhile, she was trying to calculate how much time she'd have to log on the stationary bike to burn off the calories in 1024 M&M's.

That was one equation she wasn't eager to solve.

The phone was ringing when they walked into the

house. Cecilia picked up the cordless in the kitchen. "Hello?"

"Cece, it's me."

"Dannie?"

"Yeah. Listen, I need a favor."

"Okay. What's going on?"

"I need you to—" Cecilia heard screaming in the background. "Wait a second…"

Cecilia walked back into the hallway, half listening to Dannie yell at Richard for stuffing a waffle into the DVD player.

Brian stood just inside the door, quiet and unmoving, and for a nanosecond—a dark, regretful nanosecond—she wished Brian would put a waffle in the DVD player, just once.

She wished he would laugh and play baseball with the neighborhood kids and hug her spontaneously.

She held her hand over the phone's mouthpiece. "It's okay, honey. You can go up to your room if you want." She gave him a gentle nudge on the shoulder and picked up his small suitcase, following him up the stairs.

"All right. I'm back." Dannie sounded breathless.

Then again, Dannie always sounded breathless.

"What do you need?" Cecilia asked.

"I need someone to take Quincy for a couple of days."

"Quincy?" Cecilia ran through Dannie's kids names in her mind. Quincy wasn't there. "Who's Quincy?"

"My dog."

Before Cecilia could say anything, Dannie rushed on.

"I've got to go out of town. It's an emergency. My mother-in-law is going to take the kids, but she's allergic to the dog. Or so she says."

"I don't know—"

"Please, Cece. You've always been a dog lover. Quincy is great. You'll adore him!"

"I'll adore him, huh?"

"Absolutely. And you know I wouldn't ask unless it was an emergency."

Cecilia thought about Brian asking for a puppy. Maybe this would be a good way to see how he would handle an animal in the house.

"For a couple of days?" Cecilia said.

"Right. Two, maybe three, tops."

"Okay. What the hell. Ben's coming over for dinner and he hates dogs. Besides, I'll be home most of the weekend with Brian. Bring him over."

"Great! Thank you so much. I'll see you in a couple of hours."

Cecilia left Brian alone in his room to get reacquainted with his things—which remained exactly as he had left them a month and a half ago when he'd gone off to school—and went back downstairs.

She dialed Ben's mother's number.

When Ben answered, she said, "Well? Are you coming over?"

"Why? Was I supposed to?"

She counted to ten under her breath. "Yes, you were supposed to. I'm making a roast for dinner. Brian's here."

"Brian's there?"

"Yes, he is. I told you two weeks ago I was bringing him home for the long weekend."

"Oh, right. Great. Okay, I'll be over in a little while."

BY SIX O'CLOCK, it became painfully apparent Ben wasn't coming.

More angry than upset now, Cecilia went out onto the deck, wishing to God she hadn't quit smoking, and checked the roast she'd been cooking on the grill.

When the weather was mild, she cooked everything on the grill. Pizza. Turkey breasts. Casseroles. Chili. In a few weeks, though, it would be too cold. She always got just a tiny bit depressed when she had to move her base of operations back to the kitchen.

She loved hanging out on the deck in her bare feet, drinking a beer or maybe a Margarita, watching the sun set. Sometimes she would imagine she was going to leave all this stress behind and move to some tropical island, where she would whip up spectacular meals in coconut shells over a fire pit, and spend her life tanned, relaxed and slightly tipsy.

She and Brian would take long walks on the beach, looking for shells. She'd make necklaces out of them, and they'd sell them on the beach. Or maybe she could braid hair.

No. She'd be terrible at that.

She'd once tried to braid Grace's hair for school pictures, and Grace had ended up looking like an insane Pippi Longstocking. People probably wouldn't pay to look like that.

She daydreamed about beaches and Jake and cigarettes, and then about ways to dispose of Ben's body. And then the doorbell rang.

Cecilia made her way through the house to the front door.

Dannie stood on the step, a twin on each hip, little Betsy clinging to her skirt, Richard running circles in the yard and a Shetland pony on a leash trampling the yellow corydalis in the bed beside the door.

"Hi," Dannie said. "Are you ready for Quincy?"

CHAPTER 6

If it smells like a dog, it's gonna be a bitch to sell.

The pony rushed the door, dragging Dannie and the kids into the foyer. Dannie dropped the leash, and the animal bounded past her and into the kitchen.

"What was that thing?" Cecilia said.

"The dog. What else?"

"*That* was a *dog*? It looks big enough to ride."

"He is," said Richard. "I ride him all the time. Right, Mommy?"

Dannie plunked the twins down on the floor. "Keep an eye on them for a minute," she said to Cecilia. "I have to go out to the car to get Quincy's stuff."

"What? His saddle and feedbag?"

"Ha-ha. Very funny."

She hadn't said it to be funny.

Quincy leaped back into the foyer—a mass of writhing, shaggy tan fur—licked the twins' faces and raced into the dining room, rattling the dishes in the china cabinet.

"What kind of dog is he?" Cecilia asked Richard.

He shrugged one shoulder. "A big dog."

"No kidding."

"He's a big freaking moose," Betsy said. "That's what Mommy calls him."

Dannie came back in, dragging a ten-pound bag of Doggie Bits and a large tote filled with dog bowls, toys, biscuits, leashes and brushes.

"I need all of that?"

"Probably not. But I packed everything, just in case…"

"Just in case what? In case you don't ever come back for him?"

Dannie grinned. "You never know."

Quincy hopped, elklike, through the foyer and up the stairs.

"Uh-oh. Brian's up there." Cecilia raced up the steps after the dog and saw him disappear into Brian's room. In a few moments, Cecilia knew, Brian would be screaming. He didn't handle surprises very well.

But when she reached Brian's room, there he was, sitting on the floor with a puzzle, laughing as Quincy slobbered all over his face.

Would wonders never cease?

Cecilia watched them for a while, her heart aching with love for her son, and then went to sit beside him on the floor. "Brian, this is Quincy, my friend Dannie's dog. Do you remember Dannie?"

Brian nodded.

"Dannie asked if we would watch Quincy for the weekend. Would you like that?"

"Uh-huh. Can I take him for a walk? Ethan takes his puppy for walks."

"Of course you can. We'll walk him together."

"Can he sleep in my room? Ethan's puppy sleeps in his room."

"Umm. We'll see, okay?"

"Okay."

She left them and went back downstairs, where Dannie had Richard in a half nelson, attempting to pry a crystal Lalique ashtray out of his grasp while the twins screamed in unison on the welcome mat.

Betsy stood quietly in the corner, picking her nose.

Cecilia tickled Richard under the arms, and he let go of the ashtray.

"Thanks," Dannie puffed.

"No problem. It seems like Brian and Quincy are going to get along just fine."

"Good. Great. Where's Ben? I thought he was coming for dinner."

"He never showed up."

"Maybe he's just late. Out getting a present for Brian, or something," Dannie said.

"Sure. And while he's at it, he'll probably run into Johnny Depp and bring him home for dinner."

Dannie raised her eyebrows.

"Hey, if we're going to have a fantasy here, it may as well be a good one."

"Gotcha." Dannie picked up the twins and tucked one under each arm. "By the way, whatever you do, don't leave Quincy alone. He eats things. He has a preference for shiny metal objects."

"Okay. So what am I supposed to do with him when I have to leave the house?"

Dannie shrugged. "Take him with you." She bussed Cecilia on the cheek. "Listen, I really appreciate this. I hope he won't be too much trouble."

From upstairs they heard a crash and a thump.

Cecilia felt a shooting pain behind her right eye. "I'm sure he won't be any trouble at all," she said.

CECILIA LAY like a deflated birthday balloon on the family room couch after a very long evening with Quincy and Brian, who were both finally asleep on Brian's bed.

She heard the front door open, and a few moments later Ben walked into the kitchen.

She really should have had the locks changed.

"Where were you?" she said.

Ben shrugged.

She sat up. "Brian was asking about you all evening. Wondering where you were."

"Yeah, well. Something came up."

"Like what? What could be more important than this?"

"Lay off, Cecilia. I couldn't make it, okay? I have a lot on my plate."

Cecilia followed Ben into the kitchen. He took a beer out of the refrigerator, twisted the cap off and flicked it into the sink—a behavior that dated back to his days as a bachelor. Once when they were dating, she'd found twenty-seven beer caps in his sink. He hadn't actually washed a dish in it for three weeks.

That should have told her something about his motivation level.

"I don't get you," she said. "What could possibly be more important than your son coming home?"

Ben leaned a hip against the counter and took a swig of his beer. "I just…I didn't want to see him, okay?"

The moisture completely evaporated from Cecilia's mouth. "You *what?*"

"I didn't want to see him. I don't know what to say to him. How to act."

"You act like his father."

Ben shook his head. "You know damn well that doesn't work with Brian."

"Because you yell at him for things he can't help. He's just…he's different. He's sensitive."

Ben looked down at his shoes. "I can't do it, Cece."

The blood pulsed behind Cecilia's eyes. Coursed through her veins. This had to be what David Banner felt like just before he turned into the Incredible Hulk and twisted a city bus into a piece of modern art. "Jesus, Ben. He's your *son*."

Ben was silent.

She rubbed her temples. "What am I supposed to say to all of this? I don't understand."

He headed for the family room, but she grabbed his sleeve.

"Do you want me to say, 'Okay, you don't have to deal with this. You can just disappear whenever your son comes to town.' Is that what you want me to say?"

"Hey, you kicked *me* out, remember?"

"Yeah, out of the *house*. Not out of your son's life."

"Unfortunately," Ben muttered under his breath.

The room lurched. The floor shifted beneath her feet. Was she turning green yet? She glared at him, unable to believe what had come out of his mouth.

"What?" He took a seat on the couch and put his feet up on the coffee table.

This was the man she'd given up her freedom and her faith for. Given up her time and money and a marginally exciting sex life for. And she realized she just didn't know him anymore.

Had she ever?

The thought nauseated her.

"What?" he said again.

She closed her eyes. "Just go away."

THE REST OF THE WEEKEND passed by in a blur of keeping Quincy's nose out of the trash can, his paws out of the flowerbeds, his face out of the toilet.

Jake had spent most of Saturday there, watching Quincy and Brian while Cecilia finished up some paperwork or met a client to show a house.

"Isn't there something you'd rather be doing?" Cecilia asked him. "You know, babysitting isn't in your job description."

"I'm not babysitting, I'm hanging out with my bud, Brian."

"That's nice. Really. But don't you have a girlfriend or something?"

Jake smiled. "Not at the moment, but I'm working on it."

Cecilia envied the girl.

When she wasn't working, she and Brian did all the things he liked best, and each minute she spent with him was more precious to her than anything else she could imagine. How could Ben just walk away from this?

She imagined her thirty-nine-year-old husband sleeping in his old bedroom, still decorated with black-light posters of Metallica and the same green-plaid bedspread he once made out with the girls from Hebrew school on.

Until now, Cecilia hadn't allowed herself to think about what their separation meant. How she would handle his absence in her life after twelve years of marriage.

She supposed in some dark recess of her mind she

thought they'd get through this. They'd make it back to each other. But not now. She had no more illusions.

She only wanted to spend as much time with Brian as possible before she had to take him back to the Catalina School.

The time went by much too quickly, and on Monday afternoon she locked Quincy in her fenced-in backyard, threw Brian's bags in the back of the Cayenne and headed back to the Catalina School.

She managed to avoid Victor Newhouse on the way into the dorm, but on the way out he was waiting for her, envelope in hand. "This is from Mr. Weber."

She wondered what would happen if she refused to take the envelope from his outstretched, Vienna-sausagelike fingers. If she simply ignored him and walked on past. Would he tackle her out on the drive? Call the campus police and have her hauled off to boarding-school jail? The envelope hovered there between them.

Of course she took it.

She mustered her blandest, most superior look, and slipped it from his hands with the tiniest of smiles. "Thank you."

"Thank *you*." He gave her a smug look. She wanted to smash him in the face with her Kate Spade handbag, but she was afraid it would leave a mark. On the handbag.

Out in the Cayenne, she opened the envelope.

"Dear Mrs. Katz," she read, her lips moving silently.

"We have a strict finance policy at the Catalina School. Tuition is due two weeks before each semester, with NO EXCEPTIONS. As you know, there is quite a long waiting list for admission to the school.

"If your son requires financial aid, we do have several scholarship opportunities. However, those scholarships are parceled to our students in need before the beginning of each school year, and must be applied for through our financial aid office. If you cannot pay your son's tuition by November 1, we will be forced to drop him from the roster."

It was signed, "Respectfully yours, Melvin Weber."

Respectfully, my ass.

Okay, that gave her roughly two weeks to come up with the tuition money.

Even if she sold a house tomorrow, she wouldn't have the commission check for at least thirty days. More likely ninety.

She drove herself to the nearest gas station and pulled into a parking spot. She allowed herself a two-minute sobfest before putting the Cayenne into Drive and leaving Melvin Weber and the Catalina School behind her for another week.

By the time she'd reached her driveway, she knew what she had to do.

She had to call her mother-in-law, Ruth.

CHAPTER 7

You can't reel in the big fish without the right bait.

"So, you kick my son out on his *tuchus*, and now you want to borrow money?" Ruth's raspy voice spewed forth from the phone, causing a twitch in Cecilia's eyelid.

"It's not for me, it's for Brian."

"Oh, for my grandson? The grandson I haven't seen for nearly two months because you insist on sending him to the other end of the earth for school?"

"He's in the next county, Ruth. Not China."

"It may as well be China, for as much as I see him. You know I can't drive with my cataracts."

Cecilia dug the blunt end of a ballpoint pen into the palm of her hand. "You can see him any Saturday you want. I told you I would take you with me to the Catalina School for a visit."

"The Catalina School. *Feh.* He should be home with you. You and my son."

She wanted to say, "He was home this weekend. Didn't your son tell you?" but that would definitely not get Cecilia what she wanted. In Ruth's eyes, her son was perfection in a pizza-stained J. Crew sweatshirt.

So instead she kept the conversation focused on Brian. "He needs a lot of help right now. Much more than I can give him. Special help, from people who understand his condition."

Ruth clucked on the other end. "The only condition he has is a mother with an overactive imagination."

Cecilia's head felt like it was in a vise. A vise that could only be loosened by the magic of nicotine.

She slid the trash can out from its place beneath the kitchen sink, pushing the garbage around with one finger, desperately seeking a cigarette butt.

Her frustration had just about reached maximum levels.

"You know what? Never mind. I don't want your money. You and your son can sit in that house with your shoe-leather brisket and the plastic-covered sofa cushions—" her fingers brushed something slimy in the trash, and she shuddered "—and you can complain all you want about me and the Catalina School and my job and whatever the hell else you want to complain about. But I'll tell you right now, your son is officially yours again. I don't want his day-trading ass back in this house. Ever."

She felt something that resembled a cigarette butt and pulled it out of the trash. Crap. Only a rolled-up grocery receipt covered in egg white.

She threw it back in the can.

Nothing was worth this.

She shoved the trash can back beneath the sink and closed the cabinet door with her knee, rinsing her fingers in the sink.

On the other end of the phone, Ruth sputtered like a gimpy garden hose. "You're a deplorable woman, Cecilia. Horrible. I'm glad my son is finally rid of you."

"You know what, Ruth? The feeling is mutual."

She savagely punched the off button on the phone—not nearly as satisfying as the old cord-and-cradle phones that could actually be slammed down—and chewed a stubby fingernail.

Okay. Struck out with Ruth.

Where else could she get some quick cash?

She'd sold the antiques—at least all of the ones that were worth anything—to pay the taxes last April. She'd sold her two-thousand-dollar Trek bicycle for six hundred, to pay off Ben's tab at the clubhouse. She'd sold her wedding gown to the secondhand shop to pay the electric and water bills three months ago.

The two-carat diamond in her engagement ring had long since been replaced by an amazingly authentic-looking fake. The gorgeous abstract paintings that had hung in the living room had been replaced with prints, and the plasma TV had been returned for a regular, run-of-the-mill flatscreen.

She'd officially become an episode of *Copycats*, the

reality television show that offered up tips on how to live like the rich and famous on a shoestring budget.

Only, right now she didn't even have a shoestring.

A HALF HOUR LATER Cecilia plopped down in front of the television with a very tall gin and tonic and the stub of a cigarette butt she'd found wedged between the floorboards of the deck. It had rained the night before, so she'd had to dry the butt in the oven for a couple of minutes, but that didn't take one shred of enjoyment out of smoking it.

She flicked the TV on and surfed the channels until she came across a shot of Tom Cruise in big black Ray-Bans.

Risky Business.

She smiled, remembering her conversation with Dannie on Friday night.

If only she knew a bunch of desperate teenage boys with bonds, like the kids in *Risky Business*, all of her problems would be over. She could get a few hookers, and sit back and count the money.

If only life were so easy...

The thought hit her like one of those anvils featured prominently and often in the *Road Runner* cartoons.

She didn't know any boys with bonds. But she *did* know a lot of women with stocks.

Women who were looking for a bait shop where they could get some primo worms.

And right now she was just about desperate enough to try and dig some up.

CECILIA WAS SWEATING.

Okay, so she was sitting in a sauna. But even if she wasn't, she still would have been sweating.

She was waiting for Marjorie Almswhite to get out of her yoga class. Marjorie was going to be her test run. Her maiden voyage. If she could convince Marjie to go along with this harebrained scheme, it just might work.

Cecilia wiped the sweat from her forehead with the back of her hand. She prided herself on staying cool in any situation, but this was ridiculous. Frosty the Snowman couldn't stay cool through this.

There was no way she could pull it off.

She'd just about decided to forget the whole thing, and was peeling the backs of her thighs off the wooden bench, when Marjorie stepped into the sauna.

"Hey, Cece. What's shaking?"

"Everything these days."

"Join the Jell-O club." Marjorie sat down beside her. "No offense, but you look like shit."

"Thanks."

"I saw Ben in the lounge on Saturday night."

So that's where he'd been when he was supposed to be spending time with their son. Cecilia wondered who had paid for his drinks.

"If you ask me, kicking him out on his ass was the smartest thing you've ever done. You should have seen him hitting on Gretchen. Ugh. The man has lost all taste."

Cecilia mopped her forehead with a towel. "What's everybody saying?"

"Pretty much the same thing. We're all happy for you."

Cecilia closed her eyes and let her head thunk back against the wooden wall.

"Don't sweat it." Marjorie laughed at her own bad joke. "You know these *yentehs*. They'll move on to something new, eventually. And you will, too." Marjorie waggled her eyebrows.

Cecilia sensed an opening, and dove in. "I'm too old to find something new. At least, anything new I'd *want* to find."

"Sugar, we're all too old. But we live in hope."

Cecilia stretched her legs out and wiggled her toes, trying to look casual. "I have a friend. She's throwing this party. She says there are going to be lots of men there. *Young* men."

Marjorie opened one eye. "Yeah?"

"Young men looking for, uh, *companionship*."

Marjorie's full attention was on her now. "How would she know *that*?"

"She's inviting them just for that reason, I guess."

Marjorie sat up. "Do tell."

Cecilia shrugged. "I think they're maybe looking for

women of means. You know, women who might help them pay the bills."

"Like sugar mamas?"

"Something like that."

Marjorie laughed. "You mean mimbos! There are going to be male hookers at that party."

Cecilia wiped her forehead again. Her stomach tightened into an unpleasant knot. She could not—*could not*—spew the PowerBar that had served as her lunch all over Marjorie Almswhite's perfectly pedicured feet. "Oh, Marjorie. Not hookers, really. More like…escorts. You know—handsome, interesting, cultured."

"Oh, I love it!" Marjorie exclaimed. "What I wouldn't give to see *that*."

Cecilia waited a beat.

Dear God, it's me again. Please talk me out of this. Pleasepleaseplease…

"I might be able to get you an invitation," Cecilia said. "But it would be expensive."

Marjorie narrowed her eyes and leaned back against the wall. "Well, well." She grinned. "You gettin' into a new business, Cecilia?"

Cecilia's stomach rolled. She swallowed the taste of PowerBar that had crept into her throat. "I don't know what you mean, Marjie." She stood up. "Just forget I mentioned it—"

"Now, hang on. Sit down." Marjorie grabbed her hand

and pulled her back down on the bench. "I didn't say I wasn't interested. Besides, your secret is safe with me."

Cecilia exhaled. "I need some money fast. I'm strapped, and I figured I could provide a service. One that seems to be in demand…"

"Cecilia, we're friends. If you need money, I'd be happy to lend it to you."

"No. No, I can't do that. I want to take care of myself. Fix my own problems. I just need to find some ladies who are looking for—"

Marjorie held up a hand. "Say no more. I'm in."

"Great. Good." They sat there in silence for a moment. "Would you happen to know anyone else who'd be interested?"

Marjorie laughed. "Honey, you got a pen?"

Cecilia laid out the details, and by the time she left the locker room, she had a list of potential clients in the "Notes" section of her Day-Timer, and a buzz she hadn't felt since Jimmy Duke put a No-Doz in her Coke at the prom.

But she had one tiny problem.

She had the women for this little soiree, but where was she going to get the guys?

She couldn't exactly approach the boneheads working the supermarket checkout line and say, "Hey, I overheard you complaining that you need money for school. Why don't you let me be your pimp?"

No. Nooo way.

If she was going to do this, she'd need some help.

She'd need someone with people skills. *Guy* skills. Someone who could make sleeping with sex-starved, middle-aged socialites sound sexy.

She needed Jake.

CHAPTER 8

A handshake is nice, but get it in writing.

Cecilia had been trying all morning to figure out how to approach Jake.

He was a good assistant.

Scratch that. He was the best assistant she'd ever had, and she knew what she wanted to ask him could very well ruin their relationship. After all, picking up her dry cleaning was one thing. Finding man-whores took it to a whole new level.

Since she'd talked to Marjorie at the health club two days prior, the two of them had managed to round up twenty more women willing to fork over an exorbitant cover charge to attend her little soiree. It was to be a cash-only affair, which meant no waiting for Brian's tuition money. When the party was over, hopefully she'd have enough to keep him at Catalina, at least for the semester.

But time was running short.

Brian's tuition was due in eleven days, and she needed to have the party before then.

She'd also run into a problem with venue. She couldn't

exactly host the thing at the Budget Inn. The kind of women she'd invited would expect something upscale. Tasteful.

A cheap, upscale, tasteful bordello.

Oh, man.

She felt just a teensy bit light-headed. It wasn't too late to back out of this whole mess, was it? Maybe take a part-time job at the Dress Shack instead?

Her eyes gravitated to the school picture of Brian in the homemade clay frame on her desk. He wore the tentative smile she'd seen more and more lately, much to her pleasure. A smile from Brian had been a rarity, once.

But another upheaval was sure to set him back. If he had to leave the Catalina School, who knew what would happen?

She *had* to do this. For his sake.

Jake strolled into her office, his broad shoulders encased in a gorgeous navy-blue blazer, his bright-green eyes set off by the colors in his silk tie.

All she needed was twelve of *him*, and she'd be set.

Her mind ran with that image for a moment, imagining the possibilities, until she started to feel flushed.

"Hello, Cecilia? You okay?" Jake waved a hand in front of her face. "Earth to Cecilia."

"Oh. Sorry. Just daydreaming."

"About something good, I hope."

"Mmm." She bit her lower lip.

Jake gave her the look she could never place. The look he'd been giving her a lot lately.

"What's up?" she said.

He slapped a handful of pink memo slips on her desk. "These are all inquiries on the Palmer property."

"You're kidding."

"Nope. The phone's been ringing off the hook about it."

"I can't believe it. I had no idea there would be such interest."

"Don't get excited. The news isn't really that great."

"Are you kidding?" Cecilia jumped up and grabbed the memo slips. "We haven't had a listing generate such interest in months. Years. I'd better—"

"Cecilia—"

"—return these calls—"

"Cecilia, wait. The only reason you got those calls is because the price is wrong in the Multiple List Service system. Somehow it got changed from nine-fifty to six-fifty overnight, and was automatically sent to dozens of agents and their clients."

"What? How could that happen?"

Jake shook his head. "I entered that information myself yesterday, and it was all correct when I checked it last night."

"Beverly," Cecilia muttered.

"I wouldn't put it past her." Jake plucked the messages from her fingers. "I'll correct the price on the system and call everybody back."

"Jake, wait." Cecilia grabbed his arm.

Wow, it was hard. Hard and warm and muscular... She snatched her hand away.

He turned back to her, a flash of...something...in his eye.

She swallowed involuntarily. "I wondered...do you want a cup of coffee before you start that?"

Chicken, an annoying little voice whispered in her brain. *Big, fat chicken.*

Jake nodded. "Sure. Okay. What can I get for you?"

"Nothing. I'll get it. You just wait here."

She headed off to the small office kitchen in search of beverages...and the fortitude to proposition her assistant.

About the *party*, of course.

She poured the coffee—or by this point in the day, the molten, viscous sludge—into their mugs, as she practiced her pitch in her mind.

By the way, Jake, I need you to do a couple of things for me. Update my Web site, mail out my newsletters. Oh, and find me a dozen or so hot, twenty-something guys willing to sleep with older women for money.

Hmm. Not very subtle.

Okay, how about:

Hey, I'm throwing a little party, and I wondered if you could help me out with the entertainment?

Maybe a bit *too* subtle.

Oh, screw it. She was just going to have to wing it.

As she carried the two steaming mugs from the kitchen, Beverly Banff, the bitchy upstart Cecilia had mentored once upon a time, looked up from her desk and smirked. "The boss is getting coffee for her assistant now? Interesting."

Cecilia leveled her with an icy gaze. "Oh, I'm sorry, Beverly. Did you want something? A bowl of cream, perhaps? Some catnip? Or maybe you'd like to change the price on a few more of my MLS listings."

"How in the world would I do that? I don't have your password." Beverly gave her an innocent China-doll look, all big blue eyes and rose-petal cheeks.

Cecilia sat on the edge of Bev's desk and leaned in until they were nose to nose. "I've been hanging around this alley a lot longer than you, kitten. And I know how to use my claws."

Beverly's crimson lips curled back from her perfectly straight, perfectly white teeth. "Bring it on. I'm all for a good catfight. I've got nothing to lose."

"We'll see about that."

When Cecilia returned to her office, Jake was seated in one of the black leather guest chairs, his long legs crossed at the ankles, holding the photo of Brian.

When she closed her office door, he put the picture back on her desk. "Did the little guy get back to school okay?"

She smiled. "Yep. But all he could talk about the whole way back was how he wants to get a dog."

"That's cool. I got a dog when I was about his age. It would be good for him."

"I don't know. I was relieved when Dannie came to pick up Quincy. I'm pretty sure he ate the remote control for the television in my bedroom. I can't prove it, though."

"Are you kidding? Quincy rocks."

"Quincy is as dumb as a rock." Cecilia handed Jake his coffee.

She took a deep breath to calm the butterflies in her stomach…and just blurted out what she'd wanted to say all day.

"Jake, I really need your help." Her voice shook. The cool, controlled Cecilia was slipping away. Eroding, molecule by molecule.

Jake's coffee mug stopped midway to his mouth. He set it back down on her desk, and gave her his full attention. "I gather this isn't about real estate."

She shook her head. "I'm broke, Jake. I can't pay Brian's tuition, and I need a quick influx of cash."

He studied her for a moment. "I don't have a lot of money. I've been trying to pay off my law school loans."

Her eyebrows shot up. Funny. She could picture Jake naked a lot easier than she could picture him as a lawyer. "I didn't know you went to law school."

He nodded. "For a year and a half, mostly to make my father happy. He's a lawyer. Wanted me to follow in his footsteps and all. But he won't pay off the loans because I didn't finish."

She leaned against the edge of her desk, facing him, and set her own mug down. "Actually, I'm not asking for a loan. I need a favor. A big one."

"Go ahead."

"I need you to find some men for me. Young, good-looking, preferably discreet and in need of some extra cash. You know anyone like that?"

"Sure, why?"

This is it. There is no turning back.

She blew a curl off her forehead. "Because I need to hire some escorts for a party. There are going to be a lot of wealthy women there who will pay big bucks to meet young, available men…"

Jake's stare was blank for a few moments, and then suddenly the light of realization surfaced in his eyes. His face turned three shades of red. She'd never seen him blush before.

"You mean, like…"

She nodded. "Gigolos."

"Oh. Wow."

The words rushed out of her now. She couldn't have held them back if she'd tried. "We'd split the profits between us and the guys. Fifty percent for us, fifty divided among them. We'd be partners." She gave it a few moments to sink in, then said, "We're talking premium prices. Heidi Fleiss prices. Three grand just to walk in the door. It would be a lot of money for one night, Jake. A lot."

He stood, and his fingers shot through his short, dark hair. "Wow."

"I know this sounds crazy, but I'm desperate. I have to pay Brian's tuition in less than two weeks, or he's out of the Catalina School. Ben ran through all our money day-trading, and I haven't made a decent sale in months. I *need* to make this happen."

"Wow. Oh, wow. What do you want *me* to do?"

"Just get the guys. Nice, good-looking, clean, cultured guys. I'll do the rest."

Jake rubbed the back of his neck. The tips of his ears were bright red.

"Okay, I can see this is making you really uncomfortable. I'll just find someone else—"

"No. Wait." He exhaled. "We'd be partners? Working together?"

She nodded.

"Then it's a deal."

"You mean you'll help me?"

"Sure. Why not?"

"Oh, God. Oh, thank you." She stuck out her hand. "Should we shake on it?"

"I have a better idea."

Jake wrapped her into a hug, plastering her against his chest, lifting her feet right off the ground.

A thousand tiny alarm clocks jangled all through her body.

Racing pulse? Check. Tingling body parts? Check. Butterflies in belly? Check.

Jake's dark-fringed eyes narrowed, and he drew a ragged breath. In a heartbeat, he was kissing her.

Not a reassuring peck, but a deep, luscious soul kiss she could feel in her heels. And in other unmentionable places.

She heard a faint squeaking sound, and for a moment wondered who had let a hamster loose in her office, until she realized the noise had come from *her*.

Jake's hands moved down her back until they rested just a fraction of an inch north of the illegal border crossing—close enough to make her nervous, far enough away to make her hopeful.

He drew away, leaving his arms around her waist. "There," he said. "Sealed with a kiss."

A COUPLE OF HOURS later, Cecilia let herself into the Grove house, locking the door behind her.

She retrieved the watering can from the laundry room, filled it up at the sink and proceeded to water the plants scattered in various rooms in the house. A giant potted fichus in the great room. A gorgeous gardenia in the living room. A three-tiered corner-stand of African violets in the kitchen.

Typically, this would be the job of the live-in maid, but the Groves had taken her with them to London, so Cecilia had offered to handle the mail and the plants while they were away.

Truthfully, she'd expected to be at the house far more often to show it. But she hadn't had so much as a nibble since the Hagstroms.

She had to admit, the place looked like the Playboy mansion. Tacky and audacious, and a little bit like the set of a porn movie. But some neutral paint and hardwood floors in place of the velvet wallpaper and shag carpeting would do wonders.

As she watered, Cecilia's mind wandered into dangerous territory.

Jake's kiss.

Since it had happened, she'd thought about little else. She'd tried to downplay it, not wanting to make things awkward between them since they had to work together for the rest of the day.

As if asking Jake to get her some gigolos didn't make things awkward enough.

For his part Jake had acted like nothing had happened.

So what in the hell *had* happened, anyway?

Maybe guys his age kissed their friends like that all the time. She'd once seen an *Oprah* episode where teenage girls nonchalantly reported that they were having sex with their male friends just "for something to do."

So maybe she was lucky Jake hadn't thrown her down on the desk and had his way with her, just for something to do.

Right. Lucky me.

She refilled the watering can and headed out onto the

terrace by the pool, forcing her thoughts away from Jake and The Kiss and back to more pressing matters.

Namely, Project Bait Shop.

Now that she had both the women and the entertainment lined up, she needed a place to hold the party. She'd called the nicest hotels in and around Philadelphia, but anywhere decent—and discreet—would cost a fortune. An expense that would really cut into their profit margin.

Cecilia's heels ticked on the flagstone as she crossed the terrace to a large, marble urn filled with autumn mums. She marveled again at the wonderful layout of the place and wondered why it hadn't sold.

Aside from the *Debbie Does Dallas* decor, it really was lovely—

Whoa. Hold on. Wait a minute.

One party without a venue.

One huge, unoccupied house miles away from anything.

Was this not the classic no-brainer?

A line from *Risky Business* slid into the living room of her mind in its underwear:

"Don't worry, dear. We trust you. Just use your best judgment."

Mmm, oh, yeah. This would work just fine.

CHAPTER 9

Curb appeal only goes so far.

Oh, man. These guys *definitely* had curb appeal.

Half-dressed and not a single one a day over twenty-five, the men that littered Cecilia's finished basement were the stuff of fantasies. Draped over sofas and chairs, shooting pool, leaning against the bar. Tanned, muscular, sweaty.

Mercy. It was Beefcake City, and she was the mayor.

Close your mouth, her cool side whispered. *Don't drool.*

Jake, looking crisp and businesslike in a dark-gray Armani Exchange coat and black pants, spotted her from across the room. In slow motion—she would have *sworn* it was slow motion!—he came toward her. He looked yummy enough to serve on a plate.

"I know what you're thinking," he said.

He couldn't possibly.

"Is it that obvious?" she said.

"They're a little rough."

"Are they?" She sucked in a breath.

"Most of them came straight from work. But once we clean them up a bit, they'll look a lot better."

Oh, *that* kind of rough.

"Uh-huh." She muttered, thinking it wasn't possible that they could look any better.

Jake snapped his fingers in front of her eyes. "You okay? Are you disappointed? I only had a couple of days, or I might have been able to do better."

She scanned the yards and yards of tanned flesh and muscle, punctuated by the occasional tattoo, and she said, "Jake, you're my hero."

An hour later, however, after walking amongst them, she understood what Jake had meant when he said "rough."

These guys were far from the clean, educated, smooth-talking American Gigolos she'd expected. Richard Gere, they were not.

They didn't smell good, they didn't put a lot of stock into personal hygiene, and they didn't speak three languages. In fact, they barely spoke English.

She'd been "dude"-ed about a hundred times, had endured a multitude of bodily noises that had all the guys cracking up, and Jake had to break up more than one shoving match that erupted when a discussion about the trade of a certain Philadelphia Eagles running back turned ugly.

Cecilia watched them for a while, like Dian Fossey watched the gorillas, taking copious notes on their behavior and trying to figure out what, if anything, their primitive gestures meant.

Sadly, she realized, these boys did not have what it took to seduce a group of worldly, cultured women. Everyone knew that for "older" women, sex appeal started with the mind.

She caught a glance at Jake's butt as he bent over to pick up a beer bottle.

Okay, maybe it didn't *quite* start with the mind, but cerebral stimulation was definitely an important element.

When they'd all gone, Cecilia sank back into the couch and covered her face with her hands. "Maybe we should just forget the whole thing."

Jake sat down beside her and draped an arm over her shoulder. The intoxicating scent of cologne rich with balsam and sandalwood surrounded them, a welcome change to some of the odors she'd recently encountered.

The smell cocooned her in the illusion that there was someone else who could take charge, here. A manly man. A knight on a white steed. A father figure who could make it all better.

But there wasn't. There was only a man who'd been merely a boy just yesterday. This was all on her.

"I'm not going to tell you what to do," Jake said, as if to underscore her thoughts. "But the guys are pretty psyched up about the idea of this thing. All that money. Plus, you know, it's sort of a fantasy…"

"What, to be fondled by a bunch of perimenopausal women?"

Jake grinned. "To get paid for sex."

"Oh."

"Listen, they're more than willing to do this. They just need a little polishing."

"A *little?*" She shook her head. "One of them peed in the potted palm."

"Frat boy." Jake shook his head. "I used to be one of those, just four short years ago. And look at me now."

"Oh, God." He had to remind her he was only twenty-five. She removed his arm from her shoulder.

What in the hell was she going to do?

"Listen," Jake said. "We can do this. I'll help you."

She looked at him as if he were insane.

"We *can*," he insisted.

"They just… They need so much work."

"So, we'll teach them how to be good at this."

She looked at him, horrified.

His eyes grew wide. "No! No, I didn't mean the, uh, the sex thing. I'm sure they know how to do that part. I mean the other stuff. Speaking. Dressing."

"What, like gigolo charm school?"

He smiled. "Right. Exactly."

"I don't know…"

"Come on. You're the classiest lady I know. All you have to do is give them a quick lesson."

She buried her face in her hands. "We are so going to burn in hell for this."

"Well then, I guess we'd better make it worth it."

She took a deep breath. "All right. If we're going to pull this off, here's what we need to do…"

TWO DAYS LATER they were all back in Cecilia's basement. The guys surrounded her in a semicircle of folding chairs, talking to each other about sports, music and hot nightclubs. Cecilia took out the notes she'd taken the last time they'd been there.

Jake sat behind her, smelling like salvation and keeping the guys in line.

"I still can't believe we're doing this," she muttered.

"It's going to be a great party."

"I can't even think about it. I'm just going to pretend I'm planning Bridge night. A nice little card party."

"Whatever works for you." He reached out and gave her shoulders a quick squeeze, summoning instantaneous goose bumps that marched up her back.

She collected herself and gave a couple of claps.

"Okay guys, listen up. We're going to cover a few ground rules. First," she said, "no one breathes a word of this to anyone. If you do, we're all screwed. Figuratively, not literally."

A few of them got the joke. Most of them stared at her like she had a potato growing out of her forehead.

"You stand to make a lot of money," she went on. "A huge amount. But you've got to be discreet. Which brings us to our second rule. Whatever, um, *activities* you arrange with the ladies is strictly your business. It's up to you. You can take things as far as you'd like, but you're under no obligation to make things physical. You're there to make our guests feel special. How you do that is up to you."

Some of the guys snickered.

"Hey," said Jake. "This is serious business."

The room quieted.

"Okay," Cecilia said. "I brought a friend for the first phase of this project."

Jake went upstairs and returned with Cecilia's beauty technician, Felicity Farrell.

Cecilia had given her a story about how she and Jake had recruited the guys for a sexy fund-raising calendar for the Menopause Foundation. Felicity was supposed to do whatever was necessary to make them look their best.

"Holy Mother of Studs," Felicity said when she entered the room. "Put me down for ten."

"Ten what?"

"Ten of those calendars. What else?"

"Oh," Cecilia said. "Will do." She pretended to write that on her clipboard. "Okay, guys, stand up." To Felicity, she said, "So what do you think? Can they be helped?"

Felicity paced the line like a drill sergeant, inspecting their hair, their skin, their nails. "Let's start with this one."

She plucked a brunet named Rob—who had a fabulous but hairy body, and sported a thick unibrow—out of his seat.

"Come on," she said, as she marched him to the stairs. "I've got a tub of wax with your name on it."

One by one, Felicity worked her magic up in the kitchen, while Jake took a small group over to the bar to review wardrobe and grooming.

Cecilia set up shop in the far corner of the room. She was in charge of comportment.

First up on her list was a dark, lean Home Depot clerk with bedroom eyes named Francis.

"Okay, Francis. I'm going to pretend to be your date for the evening. What's the first thing you might say to me?"

He shrugged. "Hey, baby. 'S'up?"

She shook her head.

"Umm. We gotta be home in time for the game?" He grinned.

"What are you, a comedian? Get serious."

He shrugged. "I'm only joking a little. I'm really not good at conversation. I let my moves do the talking, if ya know what I mean." He made a jabbing motion with his fist.

Cecilia set down the clipboard and folded her hands in her lap. "Why don't you just start with a compliment?"

"I can do that." Francis cleared his throat. "Uh, that's a nice shirt you're wearing."

Cecilia nodded her approval. "Good. Keep going."

"It's very blue. Like your eyes."

"Excellent! Go on."

"And it, uh… It makes your rack look big." Francis grinned again. "How was that?"

Cecilia closed her eyes. *It makes your rack look big?* She felt light-headed—and not in a good way.

"Why don't you go see Jake for a few minutes?" She rubbed her temples.

She would never make it through this day.

Next up was a tall, blond, all-American type named Devon, whose pants looked about ready to fall down around his ankles. He wore Tweety Bird boxers underneath.

"So what do you do, Devon?"

"I'm a boarder, dude."

"A boarder?"

"Yeah, you know. Skateboards. I also snowboard and surf a little. But skateboarding is my true calling."

"I see. You do this for a living?"

"Sha-a. I almost made the X Games this year. I got a sponsor and everything. I don't make beaucoup bucks, but I get some sick clothes out of the deal."

"Sick?"

"Yeah, you know. Tippin'."

Cecilia gave him a blank look.

"Cool?"

"Ah! Right." She fought the urge to shake her head. Where did Jake find *this* one? "Okay, Devon. We're going to practice eating."

Devon laughed. "Dudette, if there's one thing I know how to do, it's eat."

"Yes, I noticed. But we're going to learn how to eat *politely*." She retrieved a tray of hors d'oeuvres from the bar and held it out to him. "Okay, what's the first thing you do?"

"Uh, first I ask if any of these suckers have shrimp. I'm allergic to shrimp."

A twitch flared up on her eyelid. "Okay, good. Then what?"

Devon examined the tray for a few minutes before grabbing a handful of stuffed mushroom caps.

Cecilia slapped his hand and he dropped the hors d'oeuvres back onto the tray.

"Ow! Chill, dude."

"No grabbing." She handed him a cocktail napkin. "First, you ask the lady you're with what she'd like to try."

"Uh-huh."

"Then you take one or two for yourself."

He picked up a couple of potato puffs. "Look. Who am I?" He stuffed one of the puffs in each cheek. "'I'm gonna make you an offer you can't refuse…'"

Cecilia pressed her twitching eyelid with her index finger. "Why don't you go see Jake for a little while?"

"Right. Can I take some of these to go? I didn't eat lunch, dude."

She held out the tray.

"Sweet." Devon grabbed a handful of hors d'oeuvres,

and he and his saggy jeans slouched off to the other side of the room.

Over the next couple of hours, she worked on a leaner, a belcher, and a guy named Chuck who categorically refused to look anywhere but at her cleavage.

She spent half an hour teaching a guy with sultry brown eyes and kiss-me lips named Ahmed the parts of the body in English, and another half hour instructing a busboy named Pete how to slow dance without breaking her toes.

By the end of the day, thanks to Felicity and Jake, her diamonds in the rough all looked and smelled fantastic. But they'd need a lot more polishing if they were really going to shine.

"All right everybody, good start," Cecilia said, herding them up the steps to the front door. "Work on your conversation skills and grooming, please, and we'll see you back here Thursday night at seven."

She opened her front door, and they filed out one by one, headed off to various rust-ridden muscle cars, pickups and tricked-out compacts parked along her quiet street.

Cecilia's neighbor, Mrs. Blanchick, walked past with her pug Aloysius. The dog stopped to take a dump—as usual—on Cecilia's lawn. Mrs. Blanchick carried a pooper scooper with a long handle, which Cecilia knew for a fact she never bothered to use, as evidenced by the piles of pug crap in varying states of decomposition exactly where Aloysius stood.

Mrs. Blanchick's mouth dropped open at the sight of a dozen hotties pouring from the house.

"Great. This will be all over the clubhouse by dinnertime," Cecilia told Jake, who stood behind her on the front steps.

"Who cares? You don't like most of those people, anyway."

"I know. But I still hate it when they talk about me."

"Maybe it's because what they're saying isn't juicy enough." He slid his arms around her waist.

"Hmm. You could be right. Maybe I should flash Mrs. Blanchick."

"Or maybe you should kiss me."

She immediately went light-headed. "Jake…"

He took her by the shoulders and turned her around, and because he stood on the step above her, she had to tilt her head way back to look up into his face.

She saw a flash of raw lust in his eyes. Real lust, and her mouth went dry.

So. The kiss in the office *hadn't* been a fluke.

He wanted her. Jake Eamon, her tippin' twenty-five-year-old assistant, wanted her.

It was so wrong, on so many levels.

But at that moment she just didn't care. She reached up and circled his neck with her arms, pulling his mouth to hers.

The kiss was long and slow and wet, and involved a fair

amount of noises and inappropriate touching. When they came up for air, Cecilia glanced over her shoulder.

Mrs. Blanchick stood at the edge of the lawn with her mouth open, the pooper scooper on the ground and one foot deep in a pile of pug crap.

CHAPTER 10

There's nothing like an open house to bring out the weirdos.

"Are they ready?"

"They're ready." Jake placed a light kiss on the top of Cecilia's head.

She'd been avoiding all physical contact with him since the makeout session on her doorstep the week before, a decision that was bolstered by the reaction of the women at the Boxwood Country Club Fitness Center later that night.

Mrs. Blanchick had obviously struck swiftly and without mercy.

Half the women in her kickboxing class had looked at her with naked admiration, while the other half looked as if they might corner her in the ladies' room and sew a scarlet C for "cradle robber" on her sports bra.

Some of them had sons about Jake's age, and had no doubt warned them not to wander too close to her house, lest they be sucked into her lair.

Jake hadn't pushed things, either. She figured he'd kissed

her out of curiosity, maybe, and discovered it wasn't everything he'd hoped for.

She'd be lying if she said she didn't feel just a teensy bit disappointed by that. Plus, being surrounded by all those beautiful young men had wreaked havoc on her libido.

She straightened Jake's tie, and did a final run-through on the Grove house.

The caterers would serve finger foods, and had set up hot and cold hors d'oeuvres stations throughout the house and out by the pool, as well. It was such a mild evening they hadn't even needed to light the portable copper heating lamps on the terrace.

She'd hired a bartender to set up in the great room, a piano player for the sitting room, and a harpist for the upstairs balcony. *Casablanca* was ready to roll in the media room downstairs.

There were clean towels in all the bathrooms, clean sheets in all the bedrooms, and a giant bowl of condoms in the master bath.

They had everything.

Everything but the guests.

"The limo with the boys should be here in a few minutes," Jake said, following her downstairs. "The driver just called for directions."

"Good." She took a deep breath, but it failed to loosen the knot in her belly.

Jake took her hand. "It's going to work out fine. Really.

And by the end of the night, we're going to have a pile of cash."

She closed her eyes and pictured Brian. "I hope so. Because the thought of all that money is the only thing keeping me from running screaming into traffic on the turnpike right now."

"It's going to be great," Jake said. "You look great." He gave her the once over. "What's on your shoe?"

She looked down. "Oh, crap. It's artichoke dip."

Jake got her a damp paper towel from the kitchen and she tried to wipe it off, but she only succeeded in smearing it.

"I'm going to go borrow a pair of shoes from Candy," she said.

She ran upstairs to the walk-in closet in the master bedroom, to Candy Grove's alphabetically arranged shoe section. She breathed deep the scent of leather and suede, humbled to be in the presence of such holy relics.

The big names were well represented. Prada, Stuart Weitzman, Michael Kors and Kate Spade, along with lesser known but equally spectacular designers.

How Candy could have left these babies behind was a mystery to Cecilia. Although, she was relatively certain Candy had an equally spectacular collection in London.

Cecilia gravitated toward a pair of red Jimmy Choo slingbacks with a black crystal brooch on the toe. Spectacular.

She tried them on. A little tight, but they would have to do.

As she was leaving the bedroom, the doorbell rang.

"Oh, boy. Here we go."

She hurried downstairs, where Jake was already waiting by the door.

He stepped aside. "Would you care to do the honors?"

She opened the door, and the first few bars of Muddy Waters's "I'm a Man" echoed in her head. She felt dangerously close to spontaneous combustion as twelve gorgeous mimbos filed in, combed, polished and looking like a million Euros in their rented Italian tuxedos.

One by one they entered, kissing her cheek as they greeted her. Politely. Sweetly. Without a single "Hey, dude!"

She nearly wept.

"Gentlemen, you look fabulous." She could hardly believe this was the same rag-tag crew that had sucked down a case of beer in twenty minutes, and then had a contest to see who could shoot beer nuts the farthest out of his nose.

They were real men, now. Real *hot* men.

"You look beautiful in that dress, Cecilia," Francis said, pecking her cheek.

She held her breath.

Nothing. No comment whatsoever about her rack!

"What do you think?" Jake asked, when the boys had all dispersed, seeking food and liquid fortification.

"I say forget Dr. Frankenstein. You've managed to create a dozen gentlemen out of hair gel, Armani and a bottle of Eternity for Men."

Jake grinned. "I'll take that as a compliment. I'm going to check on the caterers."

BY EIGHT-THIRTY, the place was alive with activity.

The women, who arrived in groups of two or three, were undeniably impressed with their new playmates.

Devon the skater boy had caught Marjorie's fancy, and she gave Cecilia the thumbs-up from across the room as he offered her a tray of hors d'oeuvres.

In the great room, Chuck was romancing an attractive fifty-something jewelry designer with several pounds of silver baubles and hair the color of eggplant.

Cecilia tried not to look as several couples slipped away upstairs. She still opted to think of all of this as a friendly little get-together. Bridge night, only with male hookers instead of cards.

"What do you think?" Jake came up behind her and slid an arm around her waist.

"I think it's a success." She couldn't keep the note of satisfaction from her voice.

"I agree. Some of the guys have been upstairs at least twice already—"

"Stop! I don't want to hear about it. It's none of my business."

Jake laughed. "Yes, it *is* your business. Are you still trying to pretend it's just Canasta night?"

"Bridge night." She sighed. "I just can't bear to think of myself as a madam."

"So don't. Think of yourself as an entrepreneur. Nobody's ever done this before."

"Right. Haven't you seen *Risky Business?*"

"That old movie with Tom Cruise in his underwear?"

Good Lord. That "old" movie? He must think *she* was ancient. And she guessed compared to him she was.

"Yes, that old movie." She gently removed his arm from around her waist.

"I guess this *is* something like that, isn't it?"

"It's exactly like that."

"Except you don't have Guido the Killer Pimp after you."

"No, just Melvin the Cranky Finance Officer."

"Listen," Jake said, a note of seriousness in his voice. "I wanted to talk to you about something. Come with me."

He grabbed her hand and led her out to the terrace. Marjorie and Devon were there, giggling in the moonlight.

Marjorie generally laughed a lot. But never, Cecilia thought, did she giggle. In fact, Cecilia hadn't seen Marjorie so genuinely happy since her husband had been alive.

Cecilia felt a momentary rush of satisfaction. This wasn't really such a bad thing, was it? No one here was doing anything they didn't want to do. They were all adults.

"Dude, that is *so* gnarly..." Devon's voice drifted on the

night air, and Cecilia winced. Well, *most* of them were adults, anyway.

"Let's go. We don't want to interrupt them," Cecilia whispered. She and Jake sneaked back toward the house, but not before Marjorie saw them.

"Cecilia, wait." Marjorie came toward her, and Devon headed off in the direction of the house.

"He's going to get us some more champagne," Marjorie said with a wink.

"I'll go check and make sure we have plenty on hand." Jake excused himself and followed Devon.

"Are you enjoying yourself?" Cecilia asked.

"Are you kidding? I haven't had this much fun since I accidentally put my first pair of thong underwear on backward."

"So why'd you turn them around?"

"Who says I did?"

Cecilia laughed.

"You opened a damn good bait shop, Cece. All the girls are loving it."

"We aim to please."

"I see you're mixing business with pleasure, too."

"What do you mean?"

"That sexy thing hanging all over you. Is he private stock?"

"Who Jake? Oh, no no no." Cecilia felt a blaze of heat on her cheeks. "He's not one of them. He's just my assistant at the office. Nothing's going on."

Marjorie shook her head. "If you're already paying him, what are you waiting for? He's obviously into you."

"Oh, please."

"Please what? He hasn't taken his eyes off you all night. You should go for it."

"He just watches me because he's trying to learn the business," Cecilia said. But her cheeks were burning.

"The pimp business?"

"Thanks. Thanks a lot."

Marjorie snickered. "I'm just kidding. So what's the deal with this house?"

"It belongs to a client. I've been trying to sell it for months. It seemed like a good place for something like this."

"Very private," Marjorie agreed. "And perfect with the cathouse decor."

Devon and Jake emerged from the house, Devon cradling a bottle of Moët in the crook of his arm.

Jake whispered in Cecilia's ear. "I thought we were going to talk."

"Oh, right," Cecilia said. "Marjorie, I'll catch up with you later."

Marjorie grinned. "Much later." She and Devon started off toward the garden. "Darling," she said, "I believe you were telling me about the time you took a wicked header when you busted a nosegrind on the half pipe…"

"They've been having a good time," Jake said, as he led

Cecilia into the kitchen through the French doors. "Devon said—"

"Stop! I told you, I don't want to know about it."

Jake shook his head, and pulled her through the kitchen and into the laundry room. He backed up against the washer and grabbed her hands. "Don't you want to know how much money we're making?"

"Will it be enough to cover Brian's tuition?"

"Oh, yeah."

"Then that's good enough for me."

Jake tugged her hands until she was standing between his legs. "You mean to tell me the Madame of the Million Dollar Deal doesn't want to hear about money?"

"Not at the moment."

Jake's face grew serious. "Don't lose your nerve, Cecilia. It's one of the things I love about you."

"*One* of the things?" She tried to sound lighthearted, tried to brush off his words. But her insides quivered like Jell-O on a train, and she was afraid it wouldn't be long until her outsides joined them.

Jake seemed nervous, too. His hands shook as he reached up to stroke her cheek.

"Yes, one of *many*." His fingertips slid into the curls at her temples, and he drew her face close to his, planting a gentle kiss on her lips. "I'm crazy about you, Cecilia. Absolutely insane, in fact."

"Jake, don't be ridiculous. It's this party. You're getting carried away…"

"Why don't we get carried away together?"

He kissed her again, wild and hard, and the tiny modicum of control she'd felt only a moment ago completely evaporated. Locked in the laundry room in the dark, it felt like she'd been picked by the cutest boy in school to play that preteen party game, Seven Minutes in Heaven.

Jake nibbled her upper lip, sending naughty impulses straight where the sun don't shine. His hand slipped down her bare back, and he cupped her bottom, giving it a gentle squeeze.

She gasped with delight.

He kissed so good. He smelled so good. And all around them, people were *doing* it. Women *her* age with guys *his* age.

She couldn't pretend it wasn't happening, any more than she could pretend she didn't want it to happen to her.

She closed her eyes. Maybe just for tonight she could ignore the fact that it would be wrong to seduce her employee. That pairing a hot young man like Jake with a lukewarm, not-so-young woman like her might be a sin against nature.

It had been so long since a man had kissed her like this, with lust in his heart—not to mention in other parts—that she almost didn't know what to do first.

Kiss him back, you idiot.

So she did.

And aside from her first kiss, with Jason Reese, behind the Dumpster on the playground, it was the kiss to end all kisses. Better than Rhett and Scarlet in *Gone with the Wind*. Better than Heathcliff and Catherine in *Wuthering Heights*.

This was Jake and Cecilia in *The Laundry Room*.

Jake scooped her up and sat her on the edge of the dryer. She leaned back as he kissed her again, accidentally hitting the on button. The dryer sprang to life, gearing into the fluff cycle, vibrating and shaking beneath them.

"I knew it would be like an earthquake with you," Jake joked, grabbing her legs and wrapping them around his waist.

She'd just reached for his belt when there was a knock at the laundry-room door.

"Yo, Jake. You in there?" Rob's thick South Philly accent.

"What's going on, Rob?" Jake said through the door.

"Yo, man. There's a cop at the door."

Cecilia's heart seized. She closed her eyes and held her breath.

Jake reached behind her and turned off the dryer.

"Did he say what he wants?" Jake asked.

"I'm not sure. One of the other guys answered the door, and asked me to come and get you."

"Where is he now?"

"Outside on the front walk."

"Okay." *Breathe, Cecilia.* "Okay," she said. "I'll go out through the garage and meet him at the front door."

"Do you think he saw anything?" Jake said.

"What's there to see? It's just a party, right?"

"Right." Jake lifted her off the dryer and straightened her dress.

"Do I look okay?"

"You have a piece of lint in your hair." He picked it out, and gave her a kiss. "You cool with this, or do you want me to handle it?"

"No, you get back to the party and make sure no one is panicking."

"Will do."

Jake went back into the kitchen, and Cecilia went through the garage. Just past the lawnmower, she felt a powerful urge to throw up.

She was so not cool with this.

She was so not cool with anything that had been going on lately.

Let's face it. She was so not cool at all anymore.

CHAPTER 11

Crowds always attract attention.

Cecilia rounded the house by way of a small brick path that ran from the driveway to the front door.

Sure enough, a cop with a roll of blubber hanging over his gun belt had his nose pressed to the narrow window beside the front door. No doubt he was getting an eyeful.

"Excuse me? May I help you?"

The cop waded out of the landscaping and touched the brim of his hat. "Ma'am. I'm Police Chief Avery McAllister."

She held out her hand, and he looked momentarily confused before he figured out she was offering it for him to shake. "Cecilia Katz. Is there something I can do for you?"

"I don't know. Depends on who you are and why you're here."

"I'm Don and Candy Grove's real estate agent."

"Uh-huh. Are Mr. and Mrs. Grove inside?"

"I'm afraid they aren't. They're out of the country."

He nodded. "They notified us a while ago that they were

leaving. When I saw lights on and cars out here, I thought I'd check it out."

"That's very kind of you." Cecilia took McAllister's arm and steered him toward the police cruiser parked at the end of the long drive. "I'll be sure to let them know you've been watching their house. I'm sure they will appreciate the effort. But as you can see, everything is just fine."

Chief McAllister stopped walking. "No offense, ma'am, but I can't just take your word for it. I have a residence I know should be vacant, but there's a gathering at said residence. So I'm going to need to see some identification."

Cecilia bit the inside of her cheek. "Of course. It's in my handbag in the house. I'll go get it."

"Good. And I also need to see identification from everyone else on the premises."

Cecilia's insides went liquid. "Is that really necessary?"

"I think it is." He started back toward the front door, but Cecilia grabbed his elbow.

"Sir, I've had a difficult time selling this house, so I decided to arrange this broker tour to generate some interest in the property."

"A broker tour?"

"Yes, sir."

"At night?"

"Well, yes. The property is at its most attractive at night, don't you agree?"

"I wouldn't know, ma'am."

She bestowed upon him her most dazzling smile, which, unfortunately, he couldn't see in the dark. "I guess you'll just have to trust me on that, chief."

"No, ma'am, I don't. I don't have to trust anyone. Are you aware of any illegal activity taking place within that home?"

Oh, dear God.

"Illegal activity?" It was as if someone put a giant rubber band around her chest. She struggled to take a breath. "Absolutely not."

"Good." He started toward the house again. "I think I'd like to see everyone's identification, anyway."

Cecilia was relatively certain she was going to collapse right there on the driveway. Tomorrow's newspaper headline flashed in front of her eyes:

Prominent Real Estate Agent Busted for Hosting Gigolo Lovefest.

Oh, no. No no no. It wasn't going to go down like that.

She flung her body in front of the chief, blocking the path to the front door. "I wouldn't want to tell you how to do your job, sir. But those brokers in there, they've brought along their best clients. People who are seriously considering moving into this community. Do you really want to leave this kind of impression on them?"

She sensed his hesitation and, like a jungle cat, went in for the kill. "And just imagine how upset the Groves would be if their chance to sell this house was compromised by your actions. I'm guessing they'd give their good friend, the mayor, an earful about that."

Chief McAllister put his hands on his hips. "Is that a threat?"

"No, sir, it isn't. It's just an observation. Isn't the mayor up for reelection next month?"

"Yes, he is."

"And doesn't he appoint, or *reappoint*, the police chief?"

"Yes, he does."

"Then you wouldn't want to piss him off?"

"I wouldn't." The chief spit on the drive. "But something isn't right in there."

"Everything is fine."

He shook his head. "Something seems…off. I can't put my finger on it."

She sighed. "Look, if you want to call the Groves, I can give you their number in London. But it's about five in the morning there. A call at that hour won't exactly endear you to them, either."

The chief said nothing.

"I assure you, Chief McAllister, they trust me to do what I need to do to sell this house."

McAllister stared her down for another minute before relenting. "All right. Just keep the noise down."

She didn't point out that the nearest neighbor was three miles away.

"Absolutely. Will do."

She accompanied him to his car and watched him drive away, the headlights of the cruiser cutting through the soupy fog that had formed over the rolling hills.

When his taillights disappeared, Cecilia dropped onto the dying grass of the front yard and hugged her knees to her chest, trying to stop the shaking. She had the same terrible feeling in the pit of her stomach that she used to get as a child, when she'd stood at the top of a flight of stairs and imagined what it would feel like to fall.

WHEN WAS THIS PARTY going to end?

After the visit from the chief, Cecilia and Jake seemed to do nothing but put out fires for the rest of the night.

Devon accidentally ate a shrimp puff and his head swelled to twice its size, so he had to be rushed to the hospital. Shortly after that, one of the bartenders took a champagne cork in the eye, and the caterer ran out of butter, prompting a late-night run to the convenience store.

Around one o'clock, Cecilia grabbed a bottle of champagne from the bar and headed upstairs, in desperate need of a drink, a cigarette and a few moments alone.

The door to the master bedroom was open and she slipped inside, closing it behind her. She sat on the edge of the bed and drank the champagne right out of the bottle, rooting through the bodice of her dress for the cigarette she'd bummed earlier from one of the guys.

Damn. Now she didn't have a match.

As she searched the nightstand trying to find a light, the door to the Groves' giant walk-in closet swung open. A man with bloodshot eyes, a puffy white face, and hair like greasy hanks of red yarn emerged.

He looked like Raggedy Andy on a bender.

No *way* he was one of theirs.

Aside from the bad hair, he had a wardrobe that might have come from the Dumpster behind the Salvation Army, a tattoo of a spider crawling up his neck, and a face full of piercings that called to mind her grandmother's pincushion.

She bit back a scream, and pointed the champagne bottle at him like a weapon. An '04 magnum. "Who the hell are you?"

"Who are you?"

"I asked you first."

For some reason this piece of grade-school logic worked. Perhaps because grade school was the last of his formal education.

"Name's Nigel," he said, with a distinct British accent.

Nigel? She squinted at him. He looked familiar. "Are you with the caterer?"

"The caterer. Right."

"Then shouldn't you be down in the kitchen? What are you doing in the closet?"

He gave her an amused look. "Just looking for the loo."

She lowered her weapon. "Right there. That door." She pointed with the champagne bottle to the master bathroom.

Nigel went in and closed the door, emerging a few minutes later with a handful of condoms. "Found these in a bowl in there," he said. "Are these for anybody, then?"

She rolled her eyes. "Just take them."

He stuffed the condoms in his pocket and slugged out.

Too late she realized she should have asked him if he had a light.

She took another slug of champagne, and located the remote control for the gas fireplace. She pressed a button, and *voilà!* Flames leaped from the lifelike ceramic log.

Cecilia stuck the cigarette into the flames to light it, and the entire thing immediately caught fire and withered to ash.

"Great."

She flopped back down on the bed and closed her eyes, and the next thing she knew, Jake was shaking her awake.

"Come on, Sleeping Beauty. The party's over."

She stumbled downstairs, groggy and disoriented. The place looked like it had been bombed.

Their guys, in various states of dishabille, were sprawled out on couches and chairs, and on the fuchsia shag rug in front of one of the giant fireplaces in the great room. For a moment she thought it was all a dream. Either that, or a really great porno flick.

She spied Marjorie near the door.

"What happened to you?" Cecilia said, giving her friend the once-over.

Marjorie's pantyhose dangled out of the handbag hooked over her arm, and her bra strap drooped out of her dress over one thin but well-formed bicep. Marjorie gave her a shit-eating grin.

"What's in your hair?" Cecilia said.

Marjorie picked through her disheveled coif and pulled out a maraschino cherry.

Cecilia blinked. "I don't want to know."

"Good, 'cause I don't plan to tell you." Marjorie grabbed her and gave her a squeeze. "But I will say this. If you ever decide to host another fishing expedition, count me in."

I would rather clean toilets at the ballpark with my tongue than arrange another one of these things, Cecilia thought. But she said brightly, "Will do!"

Cecilia closed the door behind Marjorie and turned back to her men. They looked absolutely wiped out. They'd shed their jackets and ties, and in some case shoes and socks. Some of them were smoking. A few of them nursed beers.

Chuck lay snoring beneath the coffee table.

Jake was the only one who still looked put together. Aside from a shade of stubble on his chin, he looked almost exactly as he had when he'd walked in the door at seven-thirty that evening, crisp and debonair. Cary Grant in *The Philadelphia Story*.

Her heart palpitated. It was so unfair. Why couldn't he be ten years older?

"Okay, guys. Time to divvy up the profits." Jake flipped the top off a shoe-box and withdrew a stack of bills so high it shocked even Cecilia. Which answered the long-pondered question: Did size matter?

Yes, it did.

And apparently, so did youth. There was something to be said for endless stamina coupled with a lack of staying power. When you were charging four hundred bucks a pop, it paid to be quick.

After seeing the cash, Cecilia wasn't so tired anymore. And neither were the guys. They sat up straight, watching silently and with mouths agape as Jake checked his records, counted, rubber-banded and doled out packets of hundred dollar bills.

"What do you think, gentlemen?" Cecilia said when he was finished. "Was the night a success?"

"No doubt," said Bob, stuffing his take into the front pocket of his pants. "Look at that bulge. I've got enough to pay off every piece of lawn equipment I bought for my land-scaping business."

"Totally," Chuck agreed. "I'll finally be able to get the student loan officer off my ass."

There was hearty assent from the rest of the guys, who gathered up their earnings and kissed Cecilia appreciatively on the way out.

Soon she and Jake were the only ones left in the predawn quiet of the huge house.

"It's over," she said, hardly daring to believe it. "And nothing too horrible happened. The world didn't fall down around us."

"It only looks that way," Jake joked.

"Wow, this place *is* a mess." She flopped onto the big leather sofa and kicked off Candy Grove's shoes.

Jake sat down beside her and laced his fingers through hers. "The cleaning people will be here first thing in the morning. I'll let them in."

"Thanks." She squeezed his hand. "I really appreciate all your help."

"Hey, it was well worth it," Jake said. "So, what do you want to do?"

"Mmm." She yawned. "I just want to go to bed."

"*Great* idea." He leaned in to kiss her, but she pressed a hand to his chest.

"Jake…"

"What?"

"We can't do this."

He drew away. "Do what?"

"This." She pointed back and forth between the two of them. "Us."

"You mean tonight or ever?"

"Ever."

"I thought we had something going," he said. "What happened?"

"I came to my senses."

"Cecilia—"

"I'm sorry, Jake, but you're my *employee*. We can't get involved. I don't want to lose you. I've never had an assistant as good as you."

Jake smiled a slow, wicked smile that hit her right below the belt. "You have no idea how good I can be."

He leaned over and licked her earlobe, and she elbowed him away. "I'm serious! I could get fired for sexual harassment."

"You haven't harassed me. Which is too bad, because I wish you would." He leaned in again, but she gave him the straight arm, struggling ungracefully to her feet.

"Jake, I like you," she said, slipping into her shoes. "And I'm flattered at your interest. You have no idea how flattered. But it isn't right. You are *way* too young for me."

"You're younger than most of the women at the party were, and I'm older than most of the guys. I didn't hear any of *them* complaining."

"I hate to point out the obvious, but those guys were getting *paid* to romance those women. I'm sure if they had a choice, the boys would have picked some nice young chippies with gravity-defying breasts and cellulite-free thighs, with names like Sierra and Amber and Caitlyn."

He shrugged. "No doubt some of them would. But not all of them. Not *me*."

"Have you taken a good look at yourself lately? You're a smart, sexy, fabulous guy with a good job and tons of potential. You could have any woman you want."

"Then why can't I have you?"

She sighed. "Let's just say I'm saving you from yourself."

He stood and straightened his tie. "I guess this isn't going to happen tonight."

"Or ever."

He gave her an indulgent look. "We'll see."

There was that irksome optimism again.

He walked her to the door. "Oh, I almost forgot." He reached into his pocket and pulled out a roll of cash the size of his fist. "This is yours."

CHAPTER 12

Money talks, but lots of money doesn't need to say a word.

Cecilia was surprised to see lights on in the finance office when she drove past the administration building at the Catalina School at noon the next day.

Since it was a Saturday, she'd had to make an appointment to see Weber, which she'd scheduled for two-thirty after her visit with Brian.

She swung the Cayenne into the parking lot. Maybe she could get it over with now. Then she could just relax and enjoy her time with her son without the prospect of facing Weber looming over her.

She took the elevator to the finance office on the second floor. The glass-paned door to the outer office was open, and the computer at the reception desk running. The door beyond it, bearing Weber's name in polished gold letters, was closed.

"Hello?"

She heard a thump from the inner office.

"Mr. Weber?" Cecilia started toward the door, but before

she could reach it, Weber's pinch-faced assistant, "Ms. Ann Diehl" according to the plaque on her desk, emerged.

"May I help you?"

"I was hoping to see Mr. Weber. I have an appointment with him for two-thirty, but I thought if he was available, we could take care of our business right now. Maybe salvage the rest of our Saturday."

Ann crossed to the desk and flipped through an open appointment book. "Name?"

"Cecilia Katz."

"Oh." She peered over the tops of thick glasses, her expression making it clear she shared the same low opinion of Cecilia as her boss. "Just a minute."

Ann picked up the phone at the reception desk, and Cecilia heard an electronic burble behind Weber's door.

Ann murmured into the phone. "Ms. Katz to see you…. Yes, I know. She's very early. Yes. Fine." She hung up the phone. "He'll be with you shortly."

Shortly stretched to not-so-shortly, and then to longly, while Cecilia read an outdated issue of *Accounting Today* and watched Ann bustle around the office, filing papers, tapping on the computer keyboard with what could only be described as brisk efficiency and lining up the corners of all the papers in the in- and out-boxes.

Finally the phone rang.

"Mr. Weber will see you now," Ann said, her tone smug.

"Thank you. And by the way," Cecilia lowered her voice

to a whisper, "the back of your skirt has been tucked into your pantyhose since you came out of Mr. Weber's office."

Ann's cheeks drained of color. Cecilia gave her a faux-sympathetic smile as she sashayed past the reception desk to Melvin Weber's office.

"I'm sorry I'm so early, but I—" She stopped short, emitting a low whistle. "My my, Mr. Weber. You've certainly got a lot of credentials."

The entire wall behind his desk, from floor to ceiling, corner to corner, was covered in framed diplomas, awards and accolades, certificates of merit, certificates of course completion, certificates of certification…. There had to be a hundred of them, at least.

The man had serious self-esteem issues.

"I'm a great believer in providing reassurance that one is qualified for the position one holds," Weber said, brushing an imaginary bit of dust off the corner of his desk.

An unbidden image of Melvin and Ann doing it on that exact spot flashed through her head. She imagined him saying, "So sorry, Miss Diehl. Can't do that one. I'm not qualified for that position."

Cecilia gave an involuntary shudder.

"Have a seat, won't you?" Weber gestured to a chair facing his desk, and slid into his own high-backed leather model.

Cecilia sat, her eyes coming level with his chest.

Lesson number one in Business Psychology 101: Always keep the competition on lower ground.

"Let's cut to the chase, Mrs. Katz," Weber said, touching the tips of his fingers together like some evil genius in a James Bond flick. "Do you have our check?"

"No, I don't have a check, but—"

He held up a hand. "Mrs. Katz, I'm sorry. I'm afraid we've given you ample opportunity to pay Brian's tuition, but now we're going to have to remove him from the roster."

"But I just—"

"Please, spare your dignity, Mrs. Katz. Begging isn't going to change anything. You see, here at the Catalina School we…"

As Weber rattled on about the financial philosophy of the school, and the need for responsible parenting and prompt payments, Cecilia reached into her handbag and pulled out a stack of hundred-dollar bills bound with a rubber band.

She set it on the corner of his desk.

Weber stopped midsentence. "What's that?"

"You didn't let me finish," Cecilia said. "I was saying I'm sorry I don't have a check. We're still having problems with our account. But I did bring cash."

Weber stared at the stack of bills as if she'd set a brick of plastic explosives on his desk. "*Cash?*"

"Yes. I hope that's all right."

"I…ah, I suppose it is. I don't think we've ever had anyone pay in cash before…"

"Well, there's a first time for everything, isn't there?" Cecilia rose. "I'd like to thank you for your patience and understanding, but I think we both know you haven't really been patient *or* understanding, have you?"

Weber stared at her, slack-jawed. "I beg your pardon?"

"You heard me." She hooked her handbag over her shoulder and leaned in. In a low voice, she said, "I don't like you, Mr. Weber. You're a certified jackass. But my son is getting a great education here, and I don't want to screw that up. So in the future, let's just try to avoid one another, shall we?"

She brushed past him, rattling the certificates on the wall when she slammed the door behind her.

SHE AND BRIAN had a great visit, feeding the ducks in the pond and sharing an ice-cream sundae at a local diner. It was made all the sweeter by the fact that she knew her son would be attending the Catalina School at least until the end of the semester.

Because she had a meeting at six o'clock, at four she walked Brian back up to his room, pointedly ignoring the hostile glare she got from Victor Newhouse as she passed the dormitory desk.

"Where's Quincy?" Brian asked when she was leaving. It surprised her. He typically didn't acknowledge any point in time that had passed before breakfast.

"Dannie came back to get him the day after I brought you back to school. Two weekends ago, remember?"

"Can we get a puppy?"

She sighed. Who knew what their lives would be like in

the upcoming months? Hell, who knew what their lives would be like in the upcoming days?

Would she ever sell another house? Would she drop over dead tomorrow?

If everything that had happened over the last year had taught her anything, it was that you never knew what the future would bring. She couldn't plan her life around what-ifs. She had to go for it.

Like Joel's friend Miles said in *Risky Business*, sometimes you've just got to say, "What the f—"

"Mom! I said can we get a puppy?"

She smiled. "Sure, honey. How about we look for one next time you come home?"

The rare smile that lit up Brian's face was worth all the sleepless nights and pee-stained rugs that puppy would bring.

She kissed the top of his head, breathing the scent of his shampoo one last time before she had to leave. It was so hard, when all she wanted to do was have him with her. Every day. "I'll see you next Saturday, okay?"

"Is Dad coming, too?"

Her throat constricted. "We'll see."

She'd never lied to him before, but she had no idea how to break the news that it was anyone's guess when he'd see his father again.

Fortunately, Brian didn't seem to care all that much. He went back to lining up the pencils end to end on his desk, and she slipped out of the room.

CECILIA SPED over the back roads of suburban Philadelphia thinking about the mess her life had become in just a few short weeks.

If she didn't sell a house soon, she was going to have to come up with an alternate plan. Maybe selling her own home. Or maybe working in the Home Furnishings department at Sears.

Filing for a divorce was a given. There was no way she could ever get back together with Ben. The money he'd blown was one thing, and his steadfast resistance to change was another. But what he'd said about Brian was unforgivable. She could never take him back after that.

They were better off without him, anyway.

Aside from ditching Ben, however, she had no other immediate plans. She supposed she would just have to see where life took her.

She just hoped it didn't take her to the crapper.

She pulled into her driveway with enough time before her appointment to take a quick shower, change clothes and grab a cup of coffee. But just as she cut the engine, her cell phone rang.

"Hey, we got a live one for the Grove house," Jake said. "Preapproved, and he wants to see it as soon as possible."

"Great. I have about an hour before the Oliveri negotiations. I'll head over there right now."

"The guy's meeting me at the office. I'll bring him over."

Cecilia backed out of her drive. "Good. Just stall him for about fifteen minutes. I want to make sure the cleaners did the job right. We don't want any telltale signs of last night's activities."

CHAPTER 13

A house can never have too many closets.

In ten minutes she was on the doorstep of the Grove house, rubbing Chief McAllister's greasy nose-print from the windowpane with her sleeve.

She stuck her electronic key in the lockbox and punched in the code, letting herself into the spotless foyer. So far, so good. Nobody would ever guess this place had doubled as a house of ill repute the night before.

She took a spin around the downstairs and then out to the terrace.

No dead bodies floating in the pool.

She headed back in to check out the bedrooms.

Beds all made, no leftover party guests in sight.

When she got to the master bedroom, she noticed something lying on the carpet near the bathroom door. She bent down and picked it up.

A condom. Still in the wrapper, thank God, but it nevertheless managed to elicit a shudder of relief that the party was just a memory, now. A memory she was going to try very hard to smother, with liquor or Valium or electro-shock therapy, if need be.

She slipped the condom into her pants pocket and headed for the closet to return the shoes she'd borrowed from Candy Grove's collection.

She flipped on the closet light and navigated to the shoes, section C.

Hello.

In the empty shoe compartment where the Jimmy Choos belonged, in between a pair of gray suede Cordani clogs and alligator Ferragamo pumps, sat four paperback-book-size packages. Rectangular plastic bags sealed with tan packing tape.

They hadn't been there before. Most definitely not.

She'd been in that closet dozens of times. Marcia Hagstrom had practically camped out in there. And those four packages had definitely *not* been there.

The Jimmy Choos had been there.

Her breathing quickened. Her mind divided and conversed with itself.

That's cocaine.

No, it's not.

Yes, it is!

No, it's not!

Come on. You spent every Friday night from nineteen eighty-four to nineteen eighty-nine watching Miami Vice. *You know what cocaine looks like!*

Maybe it's baby powder or something.

Right. And who put it there? One of the babies who was at the party last night?

The closet spun. Cecilia dropped to the floor and lay flat on her back, closing her eyes and hoping the packages would disappear. Maybe the cocaine fairy would come and just take them away.

But when she opened her eyes again, they were still there.

Well, it *was* the "C" section.

She struggled to her feet and picked up two of the bricks, weighing them in her hands.

Kilos, she guessed.

At least, that's what she remembered from *The Vice*.

She was tempted to cut one open with her nail file and take a little taste, like Crockett always did, but she would have had absolutely no idea if she were tasting cocaine or baby powder, since she'd never tasted either one before.

She put the packages back on the shoe shelf and opened her cell phone with shaking hands, pressing number one on her speed dial.

Damn. Jake's voice mail.

"It's me," she said. "Don't bring anyone to the Grove house. We have a problem."

The moment she finished the message, the doorbell rang.

Perfect. Just perfect.

She flew down the stairs and intercepted Jake in the hall,

where he introduced her to a square man with curly blond hair, a yellow complexion and bulging blue eyes. Sponge-Bob in human form.

"Cecilia, this is Damon Rudley."

She flashed Jake a wide-eyed, I-need-to-talk-to-you look, and then pasted a smile on her face. "Hello. Welcome. I'm Cecilia Katz." She held out her hand.

Rudley didn't bother to shake it. He strolled into the house, giving the hallway only a cursory glance.

"Mr. Rudley, please have a look around. If you'll excuse us for just a moment, I need to speak with my assistant…"

Rudley nodded and wandered off. When he was out of earshot, Cecilia clutched Jake's shoulders.

"I tried to call you," she whispered frantically. "I got your voice mail."

"I was on the phone with Devon," Jake said. "Wanted to find out how the shrimp allergy thing turned out. He says his head is still the size of a beach ball, but otherwise he's okay."

"Good to hear. But right now we've got a problem that's a little bit bigger than Devon's head," she hissed. "The cleanup crew didn't do a very good job."

"It looks okay to me," Jake said.

Rudley reappeared. Cecilia resurrected The Smile. "Mr. Rudley, have you seen the kitchen? Well, you must! It's just fabulous."

She steered Rudley to the cavernous kitchen, then dragged Jake by the sleeve into the dining room.

"What's the matter with you?" he said. "You never leave a client alone like this."

"I found a little something in the upstairs closet."

"Yeah? What?"

She peeked her head around the corner. Rudley was scrutinizing the commercial-grade gas stove.

She brought her gaze back to Jake. "Cocaine," she whispered.

"*What?*"

"I found cocaine. Four kilos, if I'm not mistaken. In the master bedroom in the walk-in, right next to those great alligator Ferragamos with the four-inch heels—"

"What are you *talking* about? What cocaine?" Jake interrupted.

She squeezed her eyes shut, doing her level best to pull herself together. The word *panic* was not in her vocabulary.

Then again, she'd never found a huge stash of an illegal narcotic in the closet of a client's house in which she'd hosted a gigolo party the night before.

She was so screwed.

When she opened her eyes, Jake was staring down at her with his beautiful, placid green eyes. "Come on, Cecilia. Talk to me. Don't fall apart."

Fall apart? The Madam of the Million Dollar Deal? The Ice Queen? She was instantly calm.

She checked on Rudley again, who had the refrigerator

and freezer open and stood in front of it as if he were having a hot flash, a look of pure ecstasy on his face.

"Mr. Rudley, will you be okay for just a minute?"

Rudley peered over his shoulder at her. "Is the refrigerator included with the house? I like the refrigerator."

"It certainly is. We'll be with you in just a moment."

He gave her an absent nod.

She focused her attention back on Jake, talking low and fast like a fedora-clad broad in an old black-and-white movie from the forties. "I found four kilos of cocaine, at least I think it's cocaine, in the master bedroom closet while I was returning Candy's shoes."

"Do you think it belongs to the Groves?"

"How could it? It hasn't been there any of the times I've shown the house to Marcia Hagstrom. It definitely wasn't there when I borrowed the shoes. It had to come from one of the people who were here last night. That, or else the cleaning crew from this morning."

"Is there more?"

"I don't think so. Not in the closet, anyway. But I haven't had time to look anywhere else."

"Why would someone leave cocaine in the closet?"

"How the hell am I supposed to—" She sucked in a breath. "*Nigel Lerwick.*"

"Who?"

"The guy who came out of the closet when I was up there

last night. Nigel Lerwick. He was the drummer for the Aching Loins."

"The who?"

"The Aching Loins. A band from the eighties. Their albums were produced by Don Grove. There's a picture of Nigel and Don together hanging on a wall in the media room. They were my friend Roseanna's favorite band. I should have recognized him."

"Maybe he's the one who put the stuff in the closet."

"It's a strong possibility, considering he's been in and out of rehab centers for the last twenty years."

"But why? Why would he leave it here?"

Cecilia thought for a moment. "I don't know. He must have known he'd be able to get into the house. Maybe he had a key? He must have left it here on purpose."

"What should we do?"

"Well we can't leave the stuff here. It's too risky. There are too many people coming in and out." She tapped her foot on the hardwood floor. "We'll take it to my place, and I'll call Don Grove. Find out how to get in touch with Nigel."

Jake kissed her forehead. "Sounds like a plan. What do you want me to do?"

She jerked her head toward the kitchen. "Distract SpongeBob. And whatever you do, don't let him upstairs until I get the stuff to my car."

Cecilia took the steps two at a time. She ran up to the

closet and grabbed the four packages and tried to stuff them into her purse, but they wouldn't fit. So she folded them into the bottom of her sweater and sneaked down the stairs.

Just as she reached the front door, the doorbell rang.

Before she could even think about freaking out, Jake materialized by her side, as if he had some sort of *Star Trek*-kian transport device.

"Wait one minute, then open the door," she said. "I'll get rid of this stuff and take care of Rudley." Cecilia made a U-turn into the great room. She scanned the room frantically, trying to figure out where to hide the bags.

The couch!

The big, quicksandlike couch. She could conceal a rhino under those cushions.

She stuffed the goods under one of the cushions and jogged into the kitchen, but Rudley was gone.

"Mr. Rudley?" she called.

She followed his muffled reply into the laundry room. Rudley had his head in the dryer.

"Mr. Rudley, is everything okay?"

"Is the dryer included?" he said. "I like the dryer. It's big."

"Yes, the washer and dryer stay with the home. Would you like to see the pool house?"

"Does it have a refrigerator?"

The guy had a definite appliance fetish.

"It has a wine cooler. And a dishwasher."

"Oh, good! Let's go."

They walked back through the kitchen. Jake stood near the center island, looking worried. Jake never looked worried.

"What's the matter?"

She heard the toilet flush in the half bath off the hall, and a moment later Chief McAllister appeared.

Cecilia took an unconscious step back.

Last night in the dark, after a few drinks and that distracting make-out session with Jake, McAllister had looked a bit like Wimpie, the hamburger-loving fatso on the Popeye cartoons. But now, in the cold light of an overdone kitchen, with four kilos of cocaine under a couch cushion in the great room, he was a tad bit more imposing.

Okay, more than a tad. He was Mount Rushmore imposing.

"Mrs. Katz." McAllister touched the brim of his police hat. "Nice to see you again."

CHAPTER 14

If you want to be a successful agent, you've got to dress the part.

"Chief McAllister! What a surprise. What brings you here?"

McAllister glanced in Rudley's direction and then back to her. "May I have a word with you in private?"

She frowned.

"It won't take long," he said.

"I understand. But as you can see, I'm busy with a client at the moment. Might I possibly get back to you later this afternoon?"

"Never mind," said Rudley quickly. "I'll come back some other time."

"Don't be silly," Cecilia said. "You haven't seen the pool. Jake, show him the pool."

"That's okay. Really." Rudley's color went from Sunshine to Cirrhosis Patient.

"Jake, will you take Mr. Rudley back to his car, please?" she said.

Jake nodded. "Call me when you're finished here. Don't forget, you have another appointment at six."

"As I said before," McAllister drawled, "this won't take but a few minutes."

Cecilia tried her most castigating look. The one that said, "If I were your mother, I'd spank you right here." McAllister didn't even blink. He probably never even had a mother. He was probably raised by wolves.

She figured she was just going to have to humor him and get him out of the house as quickly as possible.

She sighed. "What do you want, Chief?"

He sidled past her and headed directly for the great room, straight to the sofa.

For a minute—one insane, delusional minute—Cecilia would have sworn he'd smelled the cocaine under the cushions. He really *had* been raised by wolves!

But he didn't look, he just sat. Right on the goods, as it turned out.

A patina of perspiration emerged on Cecilia's forehead. She hadn't broken a sweat outside the gym since the coed screening of *Your Body, Yourself* in hygiene class in sixth grade.

She remained standing, hand on hip, hoping if she projected enough attitude he'd give up. "Do you mind telling me what you're doing here in the middle of the day, while I'm escorting a client through the house?"

"Your client left," he pointed out.

"Yes, he did, thanks to you."

The chief removed his hat and placed it on his lap, patting down an imaginary hair on a slick-bald head. "If he left because of me, I apologize. But I really wanted to ask you a few more questions about last night."

Her knees felt just a tiny bit trembly. Okay, more than a tiny bit. She should have stenciled the word *GUILTY* in capital letters across her sweat-covered forehead and been done with it.

She swallowed. "What about last night?"

"Well, ma'am. I've finally figured out what disturbed me so much about that little party of yours."

"You have?"

"Yes, ma'am. I have."

Cecilia battled the urge to throw up. "Would you care to fill me in?"

He leaned forward, propping his elbows on his knees, and peered into her eyes as if he could read her mind. "Couture."

She blinked. Of all the words he might have uttered at that moment, that one was about seven thousandth on her list. "Couture?"

"Yes."

"You mean, like clothing?"

"Exactly."

"I'm not following you."

"Everyone at that little party of yours last night was

dressed to the nines. *Couture*. At least, that's what they call it in *Harper's Bazaar*."

"You read *Harper's Bazaar*?"

He gave her a sheepish grin. A sheep raised by wolves. "My ex-wife did. She was a nut about couture. 'Course she couldn't afford anything but off-the-rack on my salary, which may be why she left me for a plastic surgeon. But high fashion was always something of a hobby for her."

Cecilia shook her head. "I'm not sure I... What does that have to do with anything?"

"Well, those people here last night, they looked like they stepped right off the pages of *Harper's Bazaar*. Is that how they usually dress for a brokers' tour? Tuxedos and fancy dresses?"

"It's not unusual." Oh, boy. *That* was a doozy. She almost laughed herself.

"Really? It's not?"

She shrugged. "It was an evening event."

"Uh-huh." The chief nodded. "Another thing I noticed, all the ladies were... I guess *mature* would be the word. On the other hand, all the men seemed quite a bit younger."

A spark of righteous anger flared, bolstering her nerve. "What's your point, Chief?"

He shrugged. "You don't see that too often, I guess. In fact, you hardly see it at all. It doesn't seem to fit."

"What doesn't fit? Attractive, intelligent women passing up overweight, bald, bitter, divorced men and going after what they *really* want?"

Chief McAllister stroked a hand over his bald pate and put his hat back on. His face turned red, and he rose from the couch.

He looked angry.

But she was angry now, too. How dare he suggest that the women at her party didn't deserve the attentions of those men? That older women weren't worthy of younger guys?

His remark was a direct hit to her ego, and now she was bleeding uncertainty.

Would an affair with Jake really be an aberration? Would it make her look ridiculous?

It was so unfair.

"You know what gets me, Chief McAllister? That a doughy, fifty-eight-year-old salesman with a bad comb-over can date a twenty-two-year-old model, and it hardly warrants a blink. But you see a few 'mature,' attractive women with younger men, and right away you assume there's something unseemly going on."

"I'm just calling it like I see it, Mrs. Katz. And the way I see it, something isn't right."

"Maybe you should get your vision checked."

"Maybe I need to talk to the Groves." He scratched his ear. "Now, I can go back to the station and have my assistant track down their number or you can cooperate and give it to me."

"I'll go one better," Cecilia said. "I'll call them for you, right now."

Screw it. If she got busted, so what? She had nothing to lose at this point.

Nothing except her real estate license and her job and her reputation, anyway.

She pulled her cell phone out of her pocket, fantasizing about whipping McAllister with a pair of control-top pantyhose while she punched the speed-dial number for the Groves' home in London.

Don Grove answered the phone. In the background, she could hear party noises.

"Hello? Hello!" Don yelled into the phone.

Cecilia yelled back. "Don, this is Cecilia Katz."

"Who? What?"

"Cecilia Katz!"

"Oh, Cecilia. Did you sell the house yet?"

"Not yet. But I've had some interest."

"Good. Great. Anything promising?"

"We'll see. Listen, Don—"

"Wait. Before I forget, I have a friend who said he ran into you at the house, and that there was some sort of party going on. What's that about?"

Cecilia's mouth went dry. She glanced at Chief McAllister. He was staring at her.

"Your friend Nigel?" Cecilia asked. "Yes, I met him. In fact, I think he may have left something here."

A brief pause on the London end. "Hang on."

Cecilia heard the sounds of the party fade, and a door

close. She could hardly believe she was discussing all of this in the presence of a police officer.

"You say you found something of his?" Don's voice was more subdued now.

"Yes, I did. Something rather valuable."

"Cecilia, that isn't Nigel's. It belongs to another friend of ours, actually. And it's very important that he get it."

"No problem. I just don't think it's safe here, what with all the foot traffic."

"Cecilia, just leave it—"

"Listen, Don, I have someone here who'd like to speak with you." She handed the cell phone to Chief McAllister.

McAllister identified himself, and briefly explained his visit, and the discovery of the party the night before.

"I wondered if you were aware of that gathering, sir," McAllister said. "I was concerned because you made it clear the house would be empty during your absence."

Cecilia chewed the inside of her cheek. She wished she could hear what Don was saying. A bionic ear would have come in mighty handy just about then.

McAllister nodded, as if Don could somehow see him through the phone. "I see. Yes. Thank you, Mr. Grove."

He handed the phone back to Cecilia.

"Don?"

"Cecilia. We're going to have to talk again soon. *Very* soon."

"Absolutely. I'm sure we'll sell it soon. What would you like me to do in the meantime?"

"Just take what Nigel left there and keep it in a safe place. I'll give him your contact information and have him get in touch with you."

"Will do. Thanks, Don."

She snapped the phone shut and looked at McAllister. "Well? Am I under arrest?" She tried to keep her tone light, which wasn't an easy feat when one was battling a nervous breakdown.

"No, you're not under arrest, Mrs. Katz. Mr. Grove assured me he has the utmost trust in you."

Cecilia clipped her cell phone back onto her waistband. "Well then, if you'll excuse me I have to water the plants. You know your way out, I'm sure."

"In a minute." The chief stuffed a meaty hand in between the cushions and rooted around.

Cecilia was about to fling herself onto his lap and wrestle him off the couch when he pulled his hand out from between the cushions. A red lace bra dangled from his index finger.

He stood, twirling the bra on his finger.

"The Groves may trust you, Mrs. Katz, but I don't. My gut says there's more to this, and my gut is rarely wrong. I'll be keeping an eye on you."

"I'm flattered I warrant such attention when there are hardened criminals out there just waiting to be caught."

The chief's mouth formed a grin that held absolutely no humor. "This is a quiet town, Mrs. Katz. There aren't many hardened criminals around, so I've got a lot of free time on my hands."

She gave him an innocent look. "Maybe you need a hobby."

He tossed her the bra. "I believe I just found one."

CHAPTER 15

Buyers are liars, but other agents are worse.

The minute McAllister walked out the door, Cecilia was on the phone to Jake.

"Where are you?" she asked, pacing the ceramic-tiled floor of the kitchen.

"I just dropped Rudley off, and I'm heading back to you. Is McAllister still there?"

"No, he just left. He made me call Don Grove in London, and told him about the party."

"What did Don say?"

"That he trusts me." She bent over at the waist and took a few deep breaths. "He also told me that Nigel was the one who dropped off the stuff. Asked me to keep it safe somewhere."

God, she needed a cigarette. Bad.

"Don't worry. I'll be there in a few minutes. We'll figure everything out."

"Right. Okay. Hurry."

She moved around the downstairs, closing blinds and

peeking out from all of the windows, half expecting to see McAllister's fat, greasy nose pressed against one of them. But his cruiser was gone.

In a few minutes Jake pulled into the driveway.

She opened the door for him, immediately comforted by the scent of his cologne and the security of his chest as he wrapped her in his arms. She closed her eyes and allowed herself a moment to feel safe.

"Guess what?" he said.

"Please don't give me any more bad news."

"No, it's good. Rudley said he was interested in making an offer on the house."

"I can't believe it. I thought for sure McAllister spooked him."

"I guess McAllister only spooked us. Where's the stuff?"

"In there."

Cecilia led him to the great room and flipped up the center cushion of the couch. She and Jake stared down into the bowels of the sofa as if they were looking into a grave.

"You sure it's cocaine?" Jake asked.

"I'm not positive. But it looks just like it did on *Miami Vice*."

"That's what you're going by? An eighties television show?"

"No. I'm also going by an episode of *Hill Street Blues*, two episodes of *Vice Squad*, and that time on *Facts of Life* when Blair got busted with an eight ball."

"Uh-huh. So you're going by four eighties shows."

"I'm just kidding. Blair never got busted with an eight ball."

"Glad to see you haven't lost your sense of humor."

"It's about all I have left, and I have to admit, it's fading fast."

"So what do we do now?"

"Get it out of here, I guess."

"You're not seriously going to move it?"

"What do you suggest we do with it, then?"

"We should flush it down the toilet," Jake said.

"I don't think so. There's too much. What if it didn't get filtered out of the water in the sewage treatment plant? The fish in every stream and river from here to the Atlantic would suddenly be flying fish. Besides, Don asked me to take care of it for him."

"But it's illegal, Cecilia. Bad stuff."

"I know that. But Don is a good client. The best I've got right now. I can't alienate him. I *need* this house. I need this sale."

Jake took her by the shoulders. "Just give it some thought, okay?"

She nodded. "But we do have to get it out of here until I figure all this out."

"So what should we do?"

"Help me find a bag or something. They won't fit in my purse."

Jake unearthed a brown bag from the pantry, and they loaded up the packages and took them out to the Cayenne.

Cecilia opened the rear hatch, and threw the bag inside.

"You're just going to leave it there like that?" Jake said. "Like an actual bag of groceries?"

"What do you suggest I do?"

"I don't know. Hide it. Put it under the seat or in that little well in the back for the spare tire."

They tried to stuff the bag in with the spare, but it created a lump under the carpet. Jake removed the inflatable tire and tossed it behind the bushes near the garage.

"There." Cecilia patted the carpet back into place. "Nobody will ever know it's there." She closed the hatch.

"Now what?" Jake said.

She sighed. "Why don't you go back to the office? I'm going to go home and wait for Nigel to call me."

"First of all, you can't go home. You have the Oliveri contract negotiations in—" he looked at his watch "—ten minutes ago. And second of all, no way. I'm not leaving you alone with this. This is half my fault, too."

"How do you figure?"

"I took half the profits from the party, didn't I?" He tipped her chin up and kissed the tip of her nose.

It was such a tender gesture it knocked all the venom out of her. She touched his cheek lightly. "That stuff doesn't have anything to do with the party. Besides, I don't want to drag you any deeper into this, Jake."

"Bullshit." He grabbed her hand from his cheek and laced his fingers through hers, pulling her close and kissing her hard on the lips. "I'm in so deep already I should have brought my water wings. But the thing is, I don't care. I love you, Cecilia."

Wow. Where did that come from?

Having the hots for your boss was one thing, but popping off The Big L? They needed to have a serious talk.

"Jake—"

He pressed his index finger to her lips. "I don't expect you to say it back. At least, not yet. I just wanted you to know how I feel."

"Wow. I just…I don't know what to say. I don't have time to address this right now, considering I have a meeting, and all this cocaine and everything."

Jake just smiled that maddening it's-all-good smile. "I'll meet you back at the office later."

CECILIA WOULD HAVE BEEN hard-pressed to say what had her more distracted—her client's ridiculous demands or the cocaine that was sitting out in the driveway off Main Street, in the spare-tire well of her car.

Then again maybe it was Jake's profession of undying love.

She tuned out the droning of the insane buyers she'd inherited from Monty and examined those last two thoughts.

First, the cocaine.

What was Don Grove involved in? Was this a one-time thing, or did he regularly use washed-up musicians to transport drugs? Either way, it was in her best interests to protect him, at least for the time being.

Damon Rudley could make an offer on the place, but if Don got busted, his house would be seized and all of her months of work and waiting would go down the drain. No commission for her.

Even though the money from the party had taken some of the pressure off, she was still one step away from bank-ruptcy.

She couldn't even think about money without breaking out in hives. So she moved on to the second question.

Was she distracted by Jake? Had he dulled her focus?

She had to admit, he had her rattled. When he had her pinned up against the dryer at the party, she'd been hotter than the permapress cycle. A few more minutes alone with him, and her delicates most definitely would have been singed.

But sexual attraction was one thing, and confessions of love were another. Even if she *were* ready for a relation-ship—which she definitely wasn't—it couldn't be with him.

Not that she didn't care about Jake. She did.

He'd been a good friend to her through her separation from Ben, always willing to meet her for a drink or dinner. Always up for a late-night chat…

Oh, boy. Could it be possible he'd been harboring a crush on her this whole time?

Maybe it was time to cool things off a bit and get her mind back on business. And she could start with the business at hand.

She sighed, and tuned back in to the conversation just as her clients were asking if they could request to have all the lightbulbs in the house changed before settlement.

Damn, she needed a smoke.

BY THE TIME Cecilia reached the office, there were only three people left. Jake, the scheduler Michael and Beverly, who was on floor time.

"Oh, Cecilia. Here." Beverly handed her a stack of pink memo slips. "I was on phones the other day when the voice mail went down. I forgot to give you your messages."

Cecilia grabbed the memos and leafed through them.

There were several messages from the loan officer at her bank. She'd called him about the Cayenne a few times, and assumed he hadn't gotten back to her yet. Now it was too late to call.

"Thanks so much," she said sarcastically. "You didn't happen to steal any of my clients, did you?"

"They couldn't be so lucky," Beverly said. "When *is* the last time you sold a house, anyway?"

"The operative word is *house*, Bev. At least I sell *houses*, and not those cheap one-bedroom roach motels you call condos."

"At least I sell something. Besides, I understand your

signs have been camping out in some pretty low-class yards these days."

"My signs? What are you talking about?"

"We got some calls that your For Sale signs were moved," Jake said from the doorway of her office. "One of them turned up in front of the shack at the sewage treatment plant. Another one in the yard of the halfway house in town."

Beverly shook her head. "Those darn kids. I wonder why they'd do such a thing."

"Because you promised to get them beer for their next party?" Cecilia said. "Either that, or you showed them your underpants."

"Aren't those the perks you promised Jake?"

Cecilia opened her mouth to speak, but Jake shook his head. He waved her into the office, and closed the door behind her.

"Here. Read this." He pushed a paper with columns of numbers into her hands.

Cecilia scanned the papers. "What's this?"

"A list of all the agents' codes who've gone into the houses with your lockboxes on them."

"Where'd you get these?"

"I requested a printout of the log from the board of Realtors."

She frowned. "Why?"

Jake shrugged. "I had a feeling…" He came and looked

over her shoulder and pointed to a number. "See this? This is Beverly's code."

"And how do you know that?"

Jake smiled. "Let's just say a little birdie told me." He ran his finger down the list, pointing to each place where Beverly's code appeared. "She's been in the Martin place three times. Did you know about that?"

"Of course not. I have a 'listing agent must accompany' on the scheduling software. Michael should have let me know about those showings."

"Maybe Michael didn't know. If Bev picked up the calls on floor time, she could have bypassed the scheduling software altogether."

"That bitch. I'm going to kill her." Cecilia headed for the door, but Jake stopped her.

"Maybe we should just let it slide for now. We don't want to let her know we're on to her until we have more evidence. Besides, people who live in glass houses…"

Cecilia nodded. "You're right. Of course, you're right."

"We can report her later. In a few weeks, when everything calms down."

Cecilia felt a rush of grateful affection and momentarily forgot her promise to herself to keep things strictly professional with him. "I don't know what I'd do without you, Jake. Honestly."

"If I had my way, you'd never have to find out. Now, let's go back to your place and wait for Nigel to call."

CHAPTER 16

Clutter is a seller's natural enemy.

As soon as they walked in the door, Cecilia cut a hard left and made a beeline for the liquor cabinet in the dining room. She poured a tall scotch, neat, for both of them.

Cecilia's mother, God rest her soul, had given her the pretty little walnut cabinet along with *The Happy Housewife's Guide to Mixing Cocktails* as a wedding gift. It was as if she'd divined how crucial a role liquor would play in Cecilia's survival of married life.

She and Jake carried their drinks into the family room and stopped short.

"Where's the furniture?" Jake said.

It was gone.

The television, the coffee table, the leather couch. Even the African fertility statue a grateful client had given her as a gift—gone.

"Oh, my God." She sprinted through the downstairs rooms. All completely empty except for the dining room set and the decrepit grandfather clock in the hall, which was, at that very moment, wheezing out a chime for the quarter hour. "I've been robbed by someone with good taste!"

"I don't think so." Jake came into the room waving a piece of paper. "This was on the kitchen counter."

She snatched it from him.

A note, written in Ben's epileptic handwriting.

"'Thanks for not changing the locks,'" she read aloud.

For a long minute, she couldn't even move. Jake put a hand on her shoulder, but she brushed it off.

"Shit! How could I have been so stupid?"

She dropped to her knees on the flattened, but stunningly unsoiled rectangle of light-blue carpet where the sofa had once been. On the floor where an end table had been was a photograph lying facedown. She turned it over.

It was a picture of Brian in his Catalina School sweatshirt. Ben hasn't bothered to steal it. She hugged the photo to her and fought to breathe.

She'd finally reached the breaking point. The tears were coming, and when they did, there would be no way to stop them. She hadn't cried since 1997. She was long overdue.

"Jake." Her voice trembled. "I need you to go to the store and get me a pack of cigarettes. *Right now.*"

He stood there, silently oozing disappointment.

"Go!"

"Okay! I'll be right back."

She heard the muted slam of the front door through the

excess supply of blood that had rushed to her brain. She keeled forward onto her forehead, lying facedown on the carpet and dragging in big breaths of air until she gagged on a dust bunny.

This sucked *so* bad.

Through her and Ben's entire marriage, *she* was the one who had propelled them forward. She'd worked two jobs while Ben got his degree at night. She'd helped him polish his résumé and score the executive's position that would take him to the top of his company.

She'd babied him through two hernia operations, forgiven him for a one-night stand with a diner hostess, and nursed their weakened marriage through various and sundry illnesses that would have killed lesser unions.

And still, he pulled *this*. Their life together meant so little to him that he could leave her with absolutely nothing.

Her tear ducts, which she would have thought had rusted shut long ago, suddenly began to work again, and she soaked the remaining dust bunnies on the carpet beneath her face.

She straggled to her feet, limping to the kitchen to find something to dry her tears. Even the paper towel holder was gone.

The bastard had taken the goddamn paper towels.

She was sobbing into a dish towel when her cell phone rang.

"Cecilia speaking," she answered automatically.

"Oh, great! You weren't in the office, so they gave me your cell number."

"Dannie?"

"Yeah. Listen, Cece, I need you to take Quincy for me again for a few days."

"Dannie, this really isn't a good time—"

"Pleeeease, Cecilia. I really, really need you to do this. I'd take him to the kennel, but he's sort of been expelled from there. In fact, he's been expelled from everywhere but your place."

"I don't know…"

"I wouldn't ask unless it was important."

Cecilia could clearly hear a note of desperation in her friend's voice.

"Hey. Are you okay?"

Dannie's voice caught. "I have to go to Cuatro Blanco."

"The island where Roger was…where he drowned?"

"Yeah. I have to get some stuff, some documents pertaining to his death. Otherwise the insurance company won't settle on the life insurance policy."

Cecilia exhaled. "Okay. No problem. Bring Quincy over."

Hell, at least there wouldn't be any furniture for the beast to chew this time.

"You're the best."

Cecilia heard a noise at the front door.

Jake! Cigarettes!

"Listen, I have to go," she said. "I'll see you soon."

She ran into the foyer and snatched the plastic bag out of Jake's hand.

"What's this?" She pawed through the bag. "Carrot sticks? Gum? *Toothpicks?*" An awful feeling welled up in the pit of her stomach. "Jake, where are my cigarettes?"

"Don't be mad," he said, shedding his jacket and hanging it on the banister by the stairs. "I know how hard you've been trying to quit smoking. It's been over two weeks. You don't want to screw it up now, do you?"

"Yes, as a matter of fact I do. I really want to screw it up. That's why I asked you to get me cigarettes." Hysteria reared its ugly head.

"No, you don't." Jake grabbed her hand and pulled her down the hall and through the kitchen, into the empty family room. "I'm going to help you get through this without smoking."

"Not if I kill you first." She was absolutely serious. If Ben hadn't taken the knives, it would have been a done deal.

"Sit down," Jake commanded.

She flopped onto the carpet and sat cross-legged where the entertainment center had been. Jake moved behind her, running his fingers over her back and up to her shoulders, where he kneaded the knots at the base of her neck.

"Ooh."

"Isn't this more relaxing than smoking a cigarette?" He pressed his knuckles into her flesh.

"I guess so."

His hands had made her forget about smoking, for sure. But they were making her think about other things...

"Lie down," he commanded.

Oh, boy. Had he read her mind? She hesitated.

He laughed. "I'm not going to attack you. I'm just going to massage your lower back."

"We shouldn't be doing this, Jake. Besides, we have to get the stuff out of my car."

"It isn't going anywhere," he said. "Sometimes you have to take a few minutes to care for yourself. Work to realign your chakras."

She knew she should object. Make him leave. Send a message that they were strictly boss and employee. But after the day she'd had, if anyone could use some chakra realignment, it was her.

She stretched out on the carpet and closed her eyes.

Jake's hands were instruments of blissful torture, and she soon lay there as flaccid as a dead jellyfish.

"I know something else that would help take your mind off your troubles," he said.

"What's that?"

"Sex."

From his lips it sounded like some heavenly decree, heralded by white-robed angels, punctuated by a celestial burst of choir music and horn trumpeting.

Sex.

Every nerve in her body sprang to life.

Jake slid a hand beneath her blouse, tracing circles up her spine, raising goose bumps on her arms.

With a subtle skill previously known only to The Fonz, Jake unhooked her bra and pulled it out through the sleeve of her shirt before she even knew what had happened.

She sat up. "How did you—?"

"Shh." He kissed her and then drew away, looking deep into her eyes. "I want to be with you, Cecilia. Please?"

So, who would have guessed that at thirty-nine and three-quarters she could feel exactly like she had in seventh grade, when Andy Rasmussen asked her to French kiss behind the Dairy Queen and she got so nervous she almost peed in her pants.

"Jake, you know I can't. I'm a married woman."

"Maybe technically. But do you really believe you and Ben will ever get back together?"

She sighed. "No. But I took vows…"

"So did he. He vowed to honor and cherish you. Instead he treated you like dirt, blew all your money and stole your furniture while he knew you'd be visiting your son. *His* son. Is that the guy you believe you have to be faithful to?"

She'd never heard a note of anger in Jake's voice before now.

"You're too young to understand…"

"What? That you refuse to let yourself be happy?"

She was silent.

"I love you, Cecilia. I fell in love with you my first day on the job."

"Jake, you've got to stop saying things like that. You don't know what you're talking about."

"Why? Do you think because I'm younger than you I can't know my own feelings?"

"It just—" She buried her face in her hands and blew out a breath. "It just doesn't make sense."

"What doesn't?"

"That you'd want *me*. There are so many beautiful girls out there your own age."

"Exactly. *Girls*. Girls that have absolutely no idea what they want out of life. Who can't find the ladies' room in a club unless they're in a pack. Who can't sell makeup at Macy's, much less a three-million-dollar home. Girls whose biggest concern is updating their home pages on MySpace."

"Jake, those are your peers. You should be doing that stuff, too. You should be having fun."

He cupped her face in his hands. "You know what's fun for me? Spending Friday nights in the office until midnight, doing paperwork with you. Having lunch with you and watching you give the waitress an extra couple of bucks when you think nobody is looking. Listening to you talk about Brian and how much you care about him. Those things are *real*, Cecilia."

She shook her head. This couldn't be happening. Guys

this gorgeous, this smart and sexy, didn't hit on her when she *was* his age.

"You're crazy," she said.

"You're beautiful."

"You're too young for me."

"You're incredibly sexy."

"I can't sleep with you, Jake."

"That's too bad, because I'm really, really good."

She hesitated. "Really?"

"Really."

So how long had it been since she'd had "really, really good"? An even better question might be, how long until she'd have it again?

"This doesn't mean anything," she said.

"If that's the way you want it."

She pulled him down onto the floor. "Then what are you waiting for?"

A SCORCHING CASE of rug rash later, the sound of the doorbell sent Cecilia and Jake scrambling for their clothes.

It had gotten dark since they'd shed them, and Cecilia crawled around on the floor, slipping her still-buttoned blouse over her head and pulling her pants on sans underwear as she ran to get the door.

"Hey!" Dannie stood on the doorstep, the bag of doggy paraphernalia in one arm, Quincy's leash dangling from the other. "You okay?"

"Sure. Why?"

Dannie reached around and grabbed the tag at the back of Cecilia's neck. "Your blouse is on inside out."

"Oh." Cecilia's cheeks caught fire. "I…uhh…"

Jake appeared in the hallway, looking tousled and sated and unbelievably delicious.

Dannie's mouth formed an O. "Say no more."

She let go of Quincy's leash and he loped past Cecilia, charging straight for Jake.

"Hey! Quincy, my bud!" Jake patted the dog.

Cecilia smoothed her hair. "This isn't what it looks like."

"Too bad," said Dannie. "'Cause it looks like fun."

"Okay, it's exactly what it looks like." Cecilia couldn't suppress the sappy grin that spread across her face like a toxic oil slick.

She didn't do sappy grins.

"Good." Dannie dropped Quincy's bag into Cecilia's arms. "What happened to all the furniture?"

"Take a wild guess."

"Ben?"

Cecilia nodded.

Dannie shook her head. "We'll talk when I get back from Cuatro Blanco, okay?"

"Sure. Good luck."

Dannie glanced over Cecilia's shoulder to where Jake was wrestling with Quincy. "Be sure to keep him hydrated."

"You know your dog is in good hands with me."

Dannie gave her an evil grin. "I wasn't talking about Quincy."

After Dannie left, Cecilia tried to call Ben's mother's house, but there was no answer. Big surprise there.

She couldn't even drive over there, because she didn't want to be in the middle of an argument with Ben about moral behavior when Nigel called to find out when he could come by to pick up the drugs she was holding for him.

Which reminded her. She still had to get it out of the car.

"Quincy!" Jake shouted from the kitchen. The dog tore through the hall, a half-eaten chicken carcass wrapped in aluminum foil in his jaws.

"There goes dinner," Cecilia muttered, as she took off after him.

CECILIA AND JAKE SAT at the breakfast bar eating soup, while Quincy lay at their feet, a puddle of drool collecting between his front paws.

"I can't believe Nigel hasn't called yet," Cecilia said.

"Maybe we should take the stuff to the police," Jake said. "We don't have to tell them we found it in the Grove house."

She shook her head. "Chief McAllister is already suspicious. What do you think he would do if I strolled into the police station with four kilos of cocaine and told him I couldn't remember where I found it?"

"Where *we* found it. And I just don't want this to get out of hand," Jake said, brushing a curl off her forehead.

"I just want to get rid of it," she said. "I want my life to get back to the way it was."

That included Jake. Or rather, the absence of Jake—at least on a personal level.

The sex had been wonderful. Phenomenal, actually. And part of her thought she'd be crazy to cut him loose.

But she was going to have to convince him to get over his crush because, let's face it, she certainly couldn't have a relationship with him. For one thing, it would be awkward working together. For another, she wasn't sure she could keep up with him.

But most of all, it would be impossible to go anywhere together. People would stare. Mothers would scold their little boys, "Don't stare at the cradle robber, Bobby. It isn't polite."

No, she didn't really need that kind of attention.

"Jake, we really need to talk. About us."

He grinned and kissed her forehead. "It's great, isn't it?"

"Actually, I was going to say it has to end. We can't do this and work together."

"Then I'll just have to quit."

"No!" She grabbed his shoulders. "I need you, Jake. You can't quit."

"I can see you tensing up again. Your aura's getting cloudy."

He spun her bar chair around and began massaging her shoulders again.

How could she possibly think when he was doing that? She melted like a marshmallow in a mug of hot chocolate. How could something that felt this good be so wrong?

She made a deal with herself. One night of fun and then it was over. Over!

Quincy gave her a look that seemed to say, "Sure. That's gonna happen."

"Shut up," she mumbled at the dog.

"What?" Jake said.

"Nothing. Not you."

Jake carried her upstairs to her bedroom, where she discovered that Ben had taken the beautiful mahogany bedroom suite but had thoughtfully left her clothing in piles along the wall and the bare mattress lying in the middle of the room.

What a mensch.

She tried to work up some anger, but it was a little hard to do with Jake cleansing her aura.

CHAPTER 17

If a buyer isn't pre-approved, don't even let him through the door.

Cecilia awoke to Jake licking her ear, his breathing hot and sloppy.

"Mmm. Don't you ever get tired?" She opened her eyes.

Quincy stood over the mattress, panting gleefully.

"Yuck!" She wiped the dog spit from her ear and rolled over.

Jake still lay asleep beside her, snoring lightly. The curve of his jaw caught the rosy rays of sunrise, and she ran a fingertip over the dark stubble.

She never would have believed sex could be so amazing. It was as if she'd been living under a rock for all these years.

Or making love under one, considering that Ben was as heavy as a rock, and about as passionate.

But Jake… Ooh-la-la. Where had he learned those moves? Pretty sophisticated stuff for a twenty-five-year-old.

She leaned over to kiss him, but Quincy muzzled in between, licking both their cheeks.

Jake opened his eyes. "Oh, thank God it's Quincy. I was thinking your breath smelled like dog biscuits."

Quincy bounded to the window and started to bark.

"Quincy, stop!" Cecilia commanded.

Quincy geared down to a whine, pacing between the mattress and the window.

Suddenly Cecilia heard the beeping noise.

"Oh, damn! I know that sound." She leaped off the mattress and rooted through the piles of clothing against the wall until she found her robe.

She raced downstairs and out the front door, just as the Cayenne was being carted away on the back of a shiny flatbed.

She jogged out into the street, waving her arms.

Ed the tow-truck guy stuck his head out the window and waved back at her. "Your little nightie ain't gonna save you today, lady."

"Ed, please! Wait!" She yelled after him. But Ed just flipped her the finger and kept on driving.

A HALF-HOUR LATER Jake hung up the phone and shook his head. "I called a friend who works at a bank. He said he can't guarantee it, but your car will probably be held at the repo lot until the bank claims it and takes it to their auction lot."

"Will anybody look in there? Will they open the car?"

"He says probably not for a day or two. They don't have

a key, and would have to get one delivered from the Porsche dealership. The bank will take possession of the vehicle tomorrow or Tuesday if you don't pay what you owe, and then they'll remove your personal items, which you'll have to claim."

"Great. I'll just go into the bank and say, 'Hi, you repossessed my car on Sunday, and I'm here to collect my belongings. There were seven CDs, a tube of Chapstick, a handful of Chuck E. Cheese tokens, a coffee mug, and...oh! I almost forgot. Four kilos of cocaine in the spare-tire well.'"

Jake rubbed his eyes with the heels of his hands. He wore nothing but a pair of light-blue boxer shorts, and his abs bunched and flexed like rubber bands as he stretched.

"We're just going to have to pony up and get your car out of hock before they clean it out," he said.

"Did your friend say how much?"

"You have to pay the deficiency, along with any charges incurred for the repossession."

"The deficiency?"

"The entire amount you still owe for the car."

Cecilia's head throbbed. "You mean pay it off completely?"

Jake nodded. "Including taxes and the repo costs."

"Jesus." Cecilia paced the kitchen floor. "I'm doomed. That's thousands of dollars. I'll never be able to get that kind of money by tomorrow."

"You don't have enough left from the party?"

"No. I paid off Brian's tuition. What about you?"

Jake shook his head. "Paid off my student loans. Well, most of them, anyway."

She pressed a palm to her forehead. "I can't believe this. Why didn't I get that stuff out of the car? What an idiot."

"It's my fault. I said it was fine."

"You're not the one who didn't make your car payments." She closed her eyes. "I really screwed up."

"It's not like you didn't have other things on your mind." He came to her and wrapped his arms around her waist and nuzzled her neck. "We'll figure something out."

She extracted herself. "Jake, it's time for you to go home. This has been fun, but I've got to get serious now."

"And you can't get serious with me?"

"Not even slightly."

He looked injured. "I want to help."

She sighed. "You can help by leaving me alone for a while. I need to think. I need to work this out."

Jake left her in the kitchen and went upstairs, returning a few minutes later wearing his clothes from the previous night. "I'm going home to change, and then I'm going into the office to check e-mail and voice mail. If you need me, just call."

His melancholy tone and wounded look were almost comical. Almost. But she could tell he really was hurt.

She walked with him to the front door. "Jake, try not to take this personally. There just isn't a whole lot you can do. I've got to figure this one out myself."

"I understand."

Quincy lay near the door. His tail thumped wildly, and he gave a happy little whine when Jake reached down to pat him on the side.

Cecilia watched Jake walk to his car and then, with an inexplicable sense of emptiness—which she tried to convince herself was due to the lack of furniture—she returned to the kitchen to make a pot of coffee so she could think.

She'd just put the filter into the machine when the doorbell rang.

Jake.

Part of her wished he could just leave this alone. But the other part was damn glad he came back.

She hurried to the door and flung it open.

But it wasn't Jake on the doorstep.

"Trick or treat."

"Nigel."

"The one and only, as my mum used to say." He shouldered past her into the foyer. "My, my. The ladies around these parts like them young. Was that your boyfriend who just left?"

Cecilia stuck her head out the door, hoping to catch Jake before he drove away.

A police cruiser trolled past, and she would have sworn it was McAllister at the wheel.

She slammed the door shut.

"What are you doing here?" she said to Nigel. "Don

told me you'd call to make arrangements for the…uh, the packages."

"Wouldn't do to have *that* conversation drifting over the airwaves, now would it, pigeon?" Nigel moved closer and touched her hair with a grubby, bloated, white hand that looked eerily like a dead trout. His eyes looked as if they should be flashing a Vacancy sign.

Why had she made Jake leave?

Cecilia looked frantically about for Quincy, who of course was AWOL the only time she'd ever needed him to be underfoot.

Nigel twirled a lock of Cecilia's hair around his index finger and smiled, showing a set of grayish snaggle teeth that could only have belonged to a washed-up English rock star.

"I do wish you hadn't got in the middle of this, pigeon."

Cecilia slapped his hand away. "Don't touch me, Nigel. I have a dog. A big, vicious dog." She whistled. "Quincy! Come, Quincy!"

They heard toenails clicking on the kitchen tile, and then Quincy rounded the corner and plowed down the hall toward them, his tongue hanging wildly from the side of his mouth, covered in dirt.

He looked absolutely insane.

Nigel's bloodshot eyes grew as big as drum-kit cymbals.

And then, Quincy completely blew the mad dog image. He emitted an excited yip and threw his undulating body at Nigel, climbing his chest and licking his face.

"Is this the vicious creature you were telling me about?" Nigel asked, scratching Quincy behind the ears. The traitor lay down at Nigel's feet and rolled onto his back for a tummy rub.

Cecilia grabbed Quincy's collar. "Don't let the happy act fool you. He'll turn on you in a second."

Quincy broke free and sped back into the kitchen.

Nigel followed.

"I'm really not comfortable with you being in my house," Cecilia shouted after him. "I'd like you to leave."

"Will do, love. As soon as I get what I came for," Nigel said over his shoulder.

She reached for her cell phone, which was nearly always hooked to her waistband, and realized she was still wearing a robe and that the phone was in the kitchen with the enemy.

Cecilia cursed under her breath, searching for a weapon in the hall closet just in case. All Ben had left was a broken umbrella and a moth-eaten fur stole her Aunt Agnes had left her. If Nigel was, by chance, a member of PETA, she could beat him to the ground with the umbrella, force him to wear the coat, and inflict some very nasty emotional scars.

"Hey, should the dog be eating this?" Nigel appeared in the doorway holding the corner of a shiny foil pouch.

Damn. She stuffed the fur back in the closet and ran out to the kitchen.

The stuff on Quincy's muzzle which she'd thought was dirt from a houseplant was, in fact, coffee.

The dog had managed to grab the bag of coffee off the counter when she went to open the door.

"I don't think a dog should have coffee," Nigel said. "Especially *that* dog. He doesn't look right."

This from a guy who looked like he mainlined espresso.

Quincy had a frenzied look in his eye. The same kind of look Cecilia got after spending the day doing paperwork and sucking down mocha lattes from the Starbucks next to her office.

"Give me that bag of coffee, Quincy," she said, speaking in a calm, rational tone.

Unfortunately, Quincy refused to be rational. He backed away, the bag of Hazelnut House Blend clenched in his teeth.

"Quinnn-ceeee…"

The dog blasted off like a short-range missile, firing himself into the family room.

"You follow him," she told Nigel. "I'm going to head him off when he comes through the dining room."

She sprinted into the hall, expecting to meet Quincy coming around the corner into the foyer. But he'd been too quick for her—no doubt aided by the caffeine—and was already on his way up the stairs.

She stalked him into Brian's room and trapped him between the hamper and a scale model of the *Starship Enterprise* Brian had made out of cardboard and aluminum foil.

"Drop that coffee," she growled.

Quincy growled back.

She dove, and ripped the bag out of the dog's mouth. Ground coffee rained down over both of them. Quincy catapulted over her and barreled down the stairs.

Man, she needed a cigarette.

She shook the coffee out of her hair and hurried into her own room, shedding her robe and pulling on a pair of sweatpants and a T-shirt before heading back downstairs.

Nigel sat at the kitchen counter, reading the newspaper and sipping a cup of tea. "Hope you don't mind. I got tired of waiting for you to come back with the coffee."

"Actually, I do mind. Can we please get this over with?"

"But of course, pigeon." Nigel set the cup in its saucer and laced his dead-trout hands over one knee. "I'll be off as soon as you give me my candy."

"Let me ask you a question. Why did you leave the stuff in that closet?"

Nigel shrugged. "Safekeeping. I had some things to take care of before I met my contact."

She opened her mouth to speak but was interrupted when Quincy tore into the kitchen and orbited the island a few times before disappearing again.

"So, love. Are you going to give me my blow?"

She shook her head. "I can't."

Nigel leaned back in his chair. "You *can't?* Why not?"

"I don't have it."

Nigel's bloated face remained passive. "I don't understand. Didn't you call Don and *tell* him you had it?"

"I *did* have it then. But I don't anymore."

Nigel's eyes narrowed. "What did you do, sell it?"

"Absolutely not. I'm not a drug dealer."

Nigel gave her a little half smile. "No, you're a madam."

His words sent a jolt through her bones. "I don't know what you're talking about."

"Of course you do, pigeon. But it's none of my business, is it? I've got my own racket."

"And what is that?"

He shrugged. "I have friends who front me money to buy some good snow in South America. I transport it to the States. I make a connection. We split the profits."

"And Don is one of your 'friends'?"

Nigel shrugged. "He and I go way back." He took his cup and saucer to the sink and rinsed them.

"How nice," she said. "A tidy drug dealer."

"This isn't *Scarface*, love. Besides, it isn't *me* you've got to worry about. It's Gordon."

"Gordon?"

"The buyer. The one who's supposed to be in possession of those cute little packages as we speak. He's already paid half of what he owes for the stuff, and he's probably got customers lined up."

"Oh."

"He's not a patient man. Waiting makes him cranky.

The last guy who made him wait got an alarm clock shoved up his arse."

Right. This wasn't going well at all.

"So, love. Do you want to tell me where Gordon's product is, or are you keen to have the ability to fart like clockwork? Personally, I don't fancy it."

She supposed there was no getting around it. She had to break the news.

"I can tell you where it is," she said. "But you're not going to be happy about it."

"Try me."

She chewed the inside of her cheek. "Don asked me to get it out of the house, keep it safe, so I put it in my car."

"Great. So let's go get it."

"We can't. I don't have my car."

"Who has it, then?" Impatience crept into Nigel's tone.

Quincy shot through the kitchen in a blur and hit the sliding glass door to the deck with a thump. He picked himself up, tail wagging and charged back down the hall.

"It was repossessed about an hour and a half ago."

Nigel gave her a blank look. "Repossessed?"

"The bank had it towed away because I couldn't make the payments, and I can't get it back until tomorrow at the earliest. That is, *if* I pay off what I owe. In full."

Nigel scratched his ear. "This is a dog's dinner, isn't it?"

"Dog's dinner?"

"A mess."

"Definitely. It's definitely a dog's dinner. But if you loan me the money to get my car out of hock—"

Nigel pulled his wallet out of the back pocket of his jeans. "How much?"

"Twenty-six thousand dollars."

"Bloody hell. I haven't got that kind of money." Nigel put his wallet away. "If I had that kind of money I wouldn't be here. I'd be at home in Chelsea, getting beaked and getting laid."

Cecilia was skeptical about the getting laid part. "Well, you tell me. What should I do?"

"Not for me to figure out, love. But whatever you're going to do, you'd better do it quickly. The clock is ticking, so to speak." Nigel got up to leave. "But I will tell you this, pigeon. Twenty-six thousand bucks is a pittance compared to what that cocaine is worth."

"Oh, yeah? What's that?"

Nigel shrugged. "Gordon already paid eighty for it. But after it's been cut and recut and distributed? Somewhere in the neighborhood of seven hundred grand."

"Seven hundred thousand…?" Cecilia's stomach roiled. "That's a dangerous neighborhood."

Quincy sped back into the kitchen and skittered to a stop at Cecilia's feet, looking up at her with wide eyes.

His expression no doubt mirrored hers. Only his was caused by an overdose of caffeine, while hers was caused by something entirely different.

Sheer terror.

CHAPTER 18

Location is everything.

"Tell me again why we brought him?" Cecilia attempted to push Quincy into the back seat, but he hovered stubbornly over the center console, drooling into the cup holders of Jake's 1990 Volkswagen Jetta.

"We brought him because we might need protection," Jake said, squinting through the blur of raindrops on the windshield. "Breaking into a repo lot probably isn't the safest undertaking."

"*Protection?* What's he going to do, lick the attacker to death?"

Quincy panted and slurped her ear.

Cecilia dug through her purse for a tissue and wiped off the dog slobber. "This is crazy."

"No," Jake said. "What was crazy was that you let that guy Nigel into your house when you were alone."

Cecilia didn't tell Jake that she thought it was him at the door. Instead she said, "I'm a big girl, Jake. I can take care of myself."

Jake pulled the car over to the curb. "Then why did you call *me* as soon as Nigel left?"

Cecilia opened her mouth but didn't know what to say. The windshield wipers slapped maniacally. "Gotchagotchagotcha."

"I called you because I... I don't have a car."

"Bullshit. You called me because you know you can count on me. Because you need me."

"No I don't—"

Jake raked his hands through his hair in a rare display of frustration. "Stop it, Cecilia. Why can't you just admit you need me?"

She looked out the window, tears welling up in her eyes. Damn. Twice in one week. The ice queen was melting.

Monty would have been so disappointed in her.

But it was so hard to stay cool, to be icy, when you just wanted to let someone else carry the burden for a little while.

A tiny sob escaped her lips.

"Hey," Jake said softly. "Look at me."

She turned, and he took her left hand, rubbing it between both of his.

"How about this? I'll admit you're a big girl if you admit I'm a big boy. Stop treating me like a kid, Cecilia. I'm a man."

She sniffed, and nodded.

"Good." He pulled the car away from the curb and began

to drive. "Okay, when we get there, Bob said to go along the right-hand perimeter of the fence off Bentley Street. He said there's a section of fencing that's falling apart, patched together with some chicken wire."

When Cecilia had called Jake earlier, he'd put out the feelers for help from the guys. It came in the form of Bob, the landscaper/gigolo, who cut the grass for the supermarket that bordered the repo lot.

Cecilia was discovering that it paid to have friends in low places.

They drove a few more blocks, and Jake parked on the opposite side of Bentley Street. The side with no streetlights.

Cecilia took a deep breath. "We're never going to be able to pull this off."

"Hey, how about a little optimism, here."

Cecilia shot him a look. Couldn't he *ever* be negative?

Cecilia pulled the hood of her jacket up. They'd both dressed in dark clothing, and she felt like a character out of *Mission: Impossible.*

"Your mission, should you choose to accept it—rescue four kilos of cocaine from an insanely expensive SUV without getting shot, arrested or peeing in pants."

"Okay, what's the plan?" she asked.

"I'm going into the lot, and you're going to watch for the cops."

"No way. I'm not letting you go in there yourself."

Jake sighed. "Why not?"

"Because, as I said before, this isn't your problem."

"I beg to differ. My fingerprints are all over those packages, too."

"So what? They're in my car, and unless you have a record, they'll have nothing to match the prints to."

Jake looked at her.

"Don't tell me you have a record."

He nodded. "Bar fight in college. I was a frat boy, remember?"

"Oh, jeez."

"So it's settled, then. We agree I have a vested interest in the outcome of this little project?"

"Agreed. But we're going in together."

"Okay, let's go."

Cecilia opened the car door. Quincy squeezed between the front seats and climbed over Cecilia's lap before she could even get one foot out the door.

"Here." Jake pulled two flashlights out of the glove box and handed one to her.

"You think of everything."

"That's why I'm a great assistant."

"Remind me to give you a bonus."

"You already did."

They crossed the street and stood next to the nine-foot chain-link fence surrounding the impound yard. Had this been the city, the fence would undoubtedly have been topped by barbed wire, but out here perhaps it was assumed suburbanites lacked the initiative to go climbing fences.

She peered through the diamond-shaped links. "There has to be a hundred cars in there."

"At least." Jake shone his flashlight along the fence and, sure enough, about halfway down, there was a hole the size of a lawn tractor patched only with some chicken wire.

Cecilia wondered if Bob had driven his mower right through the fence, and that was how he knew about the hole. Bob seemed like the type who might do something like that.

Jake pulled a pair of wire cutters out of his pocket. "Let's do it."

A minute later they pulled back a section of fencing large enough for them to squeeze through. Cecilia thought it could have been smaller if she'd gone to the gym more often that week. And if she hadn't eaten that two-pound bag of M&M's.

The rain had quit, and the repo lot was foggy and eerily quiet, like the setting of a slasher flick. Cecilia slid a sideways glance at Jake, just to make sure he hadn't suddenly donned a hockey mask or pulled a chainsaw out of his jacket.

"Why are you looking at me like that?" he asked, amusement in his tone.

"How did you see me? Do you have a third eye or something?"

"As a matter of fact, I do. I grew up near Three Mile Island, and that nuclear radiation leak had its advantages. I got a third eye. My sister got an eleventh toe. And my brother…well, let's just say he dated the ladies two at a time."

"Ooh. You'll have to introduce me."

"What, the third eye isn't sexy enough for you?"

"Can't figure out how that might do me any good."

"That's because you don't know where it is."

Their shoes sucked the mud as they methodically weaved through rows of cars. Quincy ran ahead of them, lifting his leg on every tire. He caught a scent and took off into the darkness.

"Must have smelled a rabbit," Jake said.

"Or a psychotic ax murderer," Cecilia mumbled.

They walked in and out of a few rows of cars, ducking when the occasional stray headlight flashed over the yard.

Jake said, "I know this probably isn't the best time, but can I ask you something?"

"Sure."

"Why did you put Brian in that school?"

The question caught her off guard. "Because I want the best for him. And it's the best school out there for kids with his kind of disability."

"You couldn't work with him yourself?"

"I didn't really have the time. It's very intensive, takes hours a day. And Ben had no interest in helping."

"But you could do it if you had the time?"

She didn't like where this conversation was going. "What are you saying? That I should have tried harder to keep him home? That I should have given up my job to work with him?"

Jake took her hand and gave it a squeeze. "I'm not criticizing. I'm just asking. It seems to me like you love him so much, it must have been hard to send him away."

Cecilia's throat closed. "It was the hardest thing I've ever done."

"Then why did you?"

She drew a ragged breath. "Because I was afraid if I tried to do it myself—" she swallowed, hard "—I was afraid I'd screw it up."

Jake kissed the back of her hand. "From what it sounds like, the school is great. But I think you would have been, too."

"Thanks."

They walked in silence for a while before Jake said, "There! There are some SUVS." They headed toward the vehicles parked along the side of the fence opposite from where they entered the lot.

"You have the keys?" said Jake.

"The keys?"

Dead silence. "You're kidding me, right?"

Cecilia grinned in the dark. "Yeah."

She pulled her key ring out of her pocket and it tumbled with a jangle to the ground.

Jake skimmed his flashlight beam over the ground, catching a movement at the edge of the light.

Cecilia squinted into the darkness. "Quincy?"

A silvery thing with matted, muddy fur and gleaming teeth leaped into the circle of light, snarling and keening. "Oh, my God, it's a werewolf!"

Jake grabbed her and pushed her behind him, covering her with his body. "It's not a werewolf, it's a guard dog."

"Are you sure? It looks exactly like Michael Jackson looked in the *Thriller* video, when he turned into a werewolf."

"I've never seen it, but I'll take your word for it?"

"How could you never have seen the *Thriller* video?" An edge of hysteria crept into her voice. "It's a classic—"

"Can we talk about this later?" Jake said, backing her up against a dilapidated minivan.

The beast growled and panted, moving in an ever-tightening semicircle.

"Get up on the roof," Jake commanded. "Then give me light so I can see him."

Cecilia climbed onto the bumper of the van and Jake hoisted her onto the roof. With trembling hands, she shone her flashlight down on them.

"Jesus, Jake. Be careful."

Jake wielded his flashlight like a weapon, as he and the dog faced off like bull and matador. The dog charged, and with an angry yelp leaped for Jake's throat, but Jake blocked him with the flashlight.

The dog retreated, then charged again, this time going for the knees. Jake slipped in a mud puddle and lost his balance, his body hitting the ground with a thud. The flashlight flew from his hands.

The beast moved in for the kill.

Its fangs were inches from Jake's face when suddenly, out of the darkness, Quincy charged. He hurled himself at the hellhound, snapping and growling, his gargantuan jaws closing over the guard dog's haunches.

The beast gave an agonized howl and took off into the darkness, Quincy hot on its heels.

Jake struggled to his feet, dripping muddy water. Cecilia was paralyzed.

"Come on!" Jake held out his arms.

Cecilia shinnied down off the van and they took off, running for the opening in the fence. Cecilia's lungs burned. Jake yanked her through, tearing a hole in the arm of her jacket.

Cecilia arrived at Jake's Volkswagen breathless and sick to her stomach. It was the only moment since she'd quit smoking that she could honestly say she didn't want a cigarette in the least.

It didn't last long.

"What about Quincy?" she panted.

"What an awesome dog. Did you see him attack that guard dog?"

"You mean when you were inches from death's door?

Yeah, I saw it." Cecilia's hands wouldn't stop shaking. And it wasn't just because of the adrenaline rush.

It was because for one whole minute, she'd been forced to imagine her life without Jake Eamon. And it sucked. Really bad.

She stuck her trembling hands into the pockets of her sweatshirt. "Oh, no."

"What's the matter?"

"My keys. I didn't have a chance to pick them up before that thing attacked."

"Okay. I'm going back in there," Jake said, opening the passenger-side door of the car for her.

"Are you out of your mind? Do you *want* to get killed?"

"Of course not. But we can't just leave evidence that we were in there. Besides, we've got to get Quincy."

"Maybe he'll come out," she said.

"What if he doesn't?"

She was silent. What could she say? They couldn't leave Quincy in there. Or her keys.

"All right. But please, *please* be careful."

He touched her cheek. "It almost sounds like you care."

"Of course I care. Just…hurry up."

"Aye, aye, Cap'n." He gave her a quick kiss and jogged back across the road, dissolving into the shadows.

Cecilia leaned up against the hood of the car, trying to control the erratic beating of her heart. A rumble of thunder sounded in the distance, and the damp breeze carried the faint scent of burning logs. Cecilia pulled the collar of her jacket close around her neck.

"Be safe, Jake," she whispered.

CHAPTER 19

Don't just hope to be in the right place at the right time. Put yourself there.

Cecilia was so engrossed in watching Jake's flashlight beam bobbing through the repo lot that she didn't see the cruiser until it was half a block away.

"Wonderful," she muttered under her breath.

The police car sidled up next to her, and the window rolled down. Cecilia's knees went weak, so she sat on the hood of the car.

"Why, Mrs. Katz. What brings you out at 3:00 a.m. on a night like this?" the officer said in a jovial tone.

"Chief McAllister. If I didn't know any better, I would think you were following me."

"Not me. I'm out looking for real criminals, like you suggested."

"I haven't seen any around here, but if I do, I'll let you know."

"You never answered my question, Mrs. Katz. What are you doing out here?" This time McAllister's tone was far from pleasant. He shone a flashlight in her face, and the thought occurred to her that she probably looked a lot like a criminal. Dressed in black, covered in mud, her jacket sleeve torn.

"My dog ran off. My assistant is looking for him."

"Your assistant. Is that in his job description, to help you find your dog at three o'clock in the morning?"

"We were out together."

"Uh-huh."

"He's…well, we were on a date."

The chief shifted the car into Park and let the engine idle. "Let me get this straight. You were out on a date with your assistant at 3:00 a.m., and you brought your dog? And then the dog ran away, and now the assistant is chasing after it?"

"Yes. Can you please shine the flashlight away from my face?"

The chief switched the flashlight off. "You've got a tear in your jacket."

"I fell while I was chasing after the dog."

Thunder rumbled again, followed shortly after by a crack of lightning.

Could it be a warning from the Big Guy?

She *really* had to get to confession.

Fat raindrops began to fall, splashing onto the hood of the police cruiser with a *ping ping ping*. Cecilia was getting soaked. She refused to budge, though. She wouldn't give

McAllister any reason to believe she might be guilty of something. Even if she were.

Jake materialized beneath the light of a streetlamp in the Grocery King parking lot, Quincy loping at his heels.

"Here they come now." Cecilia shuddered with relief.

Chief McAllister shone his massive flashlight across Bentley Street, illuminating a filthy Quincy, who looked a lot like Cujo, and a soaking-wet, mud-stained Jake, who had never looked better.

Jake rounded the front of the cruiser, holding on to Quincy's collar.

"Thank goodness you found him," Cecilia said to Jake. "I was just telling Chief McAllister all about how he ran off in the middle of our date."

"You told the chief you were out on a date with the dog?" Jake said.

Cecilia laughed like a madwoman and linked her arm through Jake's. "He's got such a great sense of humor," she said to McAllister. "That's what I love about him."

Chief McAllister ran the beam of his flashlight over Jake from head to toe. Jake's clothes, soaking wet from the rain, clung to his sculpted, muscled form like a second skin.

"His sense of humor," McAllister said. "Uh-huh."

The radio inside the cruiser crackled to life, and McAllister rolled up the window to answer the call.

"Did you find the keys?" Cecilia whispered.

Jake shook his head. "Too muddy. I'm sorry."

Cecilia reached over and squeezed his hand. "Thanks for trying."

Chief McAllister rolled his window back down.

"Well, honey," Cecilia said to Jake. "We'd better get home and get everybody dried off."

"Hang on," the chief said, directing his flashlight beam at Quincy. Quincy stared into the light, wagging his tail. The wag turned into a spasm, which gripped his entire body.

The three of them watched in horror as Quincy retched and convulsed and gagged.

"He's having a seizure!" Cecilia said.

"I don't think so," said Jake. "It looks like he's coughing something up."

With a thud and a jangle, something splashed into the puddle on the street between Quincy's feet. Jake reached down and picked it up. Or rather, picked *them* up.

Cecilia's keys.

"Oh," Cecilia said.

"Wow," Jake said.

Chief McAllister shook his head.

"Well, if that will be all, Chief…" Cecilia herded Jake and Quincy toward Jake's car. "Have a nice night."

McAllister narrowed his eyes. "Right."

"WHEN WE GET HOME you've got unlimited access to the trash can," Cecilia said to Quincy. "You can have a regular garbage buffet."

She scratched Quincy behind the ears, which wasn't difficult, considering that he was sitting on her lap. She figured it was the least she could do.

"What do I get?" Jake asked.

"You get a spanking. You almost gave me a heart attack."

"A spanking? I might like that."

Cecilia switched to serious mode. "We still have a problem. What are we going to do about getting the cocaine out of the car?"

"Maybe we should try to get back into the lot."

"No way. Besides the fact that we almost got killed, McAllister might still be lurking around. He isn't stupid. And tomorrow, when someone discovers that hole in the fence, we can only hope the rain took care of any evidence that we were on the lot."

"You mean besides the keys. Quincy took care of those, didn't you boy?" Jake reached over and patted Quincy's big head.

"Who would have imagined his inclination to ingest shiny objects would have an up side?"

"As would his inclination to barf them up."

They pulled into Cecilia's driveway and slogged through the now-steady rain into the house. Morning was dawning gray and dreary.

Cecilia fed Quincy some leftover lasagna from the fridge and started a pot of coffee, which reminded her of Nigel.

She checked the answering machine, and her cell-phone voice mail.

Nothing.

That couldn't be a good sign.

"We've got to get my car out of there before they clean it out," she said.

"Okay. How much do we need to pay it off?"

"Roughly twenty-six thousand dollars."

Jake gave a low whistle. He drummed on the kitchen counter with his fingers. "Hand me the phone."

He punched the buttons with his thumbs and winked at her. "Hi, Dad. Yes, I know it's early. Listen, I need a favor…"

Twenty minutes later Jake hung up the phone.

"Sorry."

Cecilia could hear a world of pain and humiliation in that one word.

She remembered twenty-five. No longer a kid, but not yet considered an adult in the eyes of parents who couldn't get past the braces and the piano recitals and the stupid mistakes of their child's youth.

Were her own parents still alive, Cecilia doubted she would even have the guts to do what Jake had just done. Call them for money.

She reached over and covered his hand with hers. "Thank you."

He nodded. "So, what are we going to do?"

She pulled him up off his bar stool and led him toward the stairs. "Let's sleep on it."

THEY DIDN'T ACTUALLY get a whole lot of sleep, and when Cecilia's phone rang at ten o'clock, she answered without her typical superagent cheerfulness.

"Cecilia," she mumbled into the receiver.

"Morning, love."

"Nigel." He sounded like he'd been on a bender, his voice rough from cigarettes, booze and God knew what else.

"You have what I need?" he said.

She rolled over so she wouldn't wake up Jake. "I told you, I have to get my car out of the repo lot. I need to get some money to get it out."

"Well, pigeon. You're a fancy real estate gal. Can't you borrow a few quid from one of your rich mates?"

"It's a bit more than a 'few quid,' and I wouldn't have any way to pay it back."

"Why would you pay it back?"

"Do you have any sense at all of right and wrong?"

Nigel laughed. "Nah. Life wouldn't be so much fun if I did."

Cecilia rubbed her eyes. "I'll get the stuff. Don't worry."

"Well, make it soon, love. So far I've managed to avoid Gordon, but it hasn't been easy. My arse is in your hands."

"What a lovely image to wake up to," she said, but the phone was already dead.

Cecilia lay on her back and pressed the heels of her hands into her eyes.

Think, damn it. Think.

Jake rolled over onto his side and nuzzled her neck. "Who was that?"

"Nigel," she said. "Remind me to pick up some Vaseline today."

"For what?"

"Apparently I'm going to need it if we don't get that cocaine back to Nigel soon."

"The alarm-clock thing?"

"Yeah." Her voice cracked.

Jake gave her a long, soulful kiss. "We're going to get your car," he said, "and all we have to do is throw a party."

She pushed up on her elbows. "Oh, no. Not on your life."

"Why not? We've got the system down, and we already know we can make enough to cover this."

"We don't have enough time to get it together."

"What do we need to get together? We have the place and the guys, and we can certainly get the clients. Everyone seemed up for a repeat performance. It just may be a little sooner than anticipated."

"I don't know…"

"A few phone calls and we can have it tomorrow night. If you collect the cover charges in advance, you'll have the money to get your car out by morning. You think Nigel could put Gordon off until then?"

Her mind rebelled, but her mouth said, "I can call him and see."

"Great." Jake crawled over her and slipped into one of her silk robes—something Ben would have died before doing.

It was great to be with a man who had no insecurities about getting in touch with his feminine side.

"What about McAllister?" she said. "He's just waiting to nail me."

"Didn't Beverly say there was some sort of rally for Mayor Sundberg tonight? Odds are McAllister will be there. Besides, as long as no one talks, he'll have no idea the party is even going on."

Cecilia chewed on her lower lip. "But what if somebody talks?"

"You worry too much," Jake said. "Why would anyone talk? They'd all be in trouble, too, if anyone found out what we're up to."

"I guess so."

"I know so. Now, get up. I'll make breakfast while you take a shower, and we'll get to work."

Cecilia flopped back onto the mattress and stared up at the ceiling fan. "I can't believe I'm doing this again."

If Dannie only knew what she'd started with her *Risky Business* suggestion.

BY THE TIME Cecilia got downstairs, Jake had a full breakfast on the table. Scrambled eggs, toast, ham, orange juice and hot coffee. It was like room service at the Ritz.

A girl could get used to something like that pretty quick.

"Wow, you didn't have to do all this," she said. "I usually just eat a protein bar or stop at the coffee place for a mocha latte."

"A perfect example of why you need me in your life," he said, scooping a spoonful of eggs onto her plate.

As she downed the first forkful, her cell phone rang. Cecilia jumped up to answer it, but it wasn't on the counter where she'd left it.

"It sounds muffled," Jake said.

Cecilia checked her purse, but the sound wasn't coming from there.

They searched the cabinets and the trash can and finally the freezer.

Cecilia had a crazy aunt who used to put everything in the freezer, and for a second she worried that she might have inherited that gene. No dice.

"It stopped ringing," she said. "Here, take the house phone and call my cell number."

The phone started ringing again. Somewhere close by.

Cecilia got down on her hands and knees, and the sound grew louder. She crawled toward it, around the kitchen island and under the table…

Bingo.

She sat back on her heels. "Naturally."

Quincy lay under the table, his wide pink tongue lolling out of his mouth, his stomach playing "Viva Las Vegas."

The sound slowed, like a dying music box, as Quincy's whole body began to quake. He snorted and heaved and coughed and gyrated until, with a strangled "gaak," he barfed her phone out onto the floor.

It landed with a soft thud in the pile of half-digested lasagna that preceded it, the green lights on the LED screen blinking spasmodically. The last notes of "Viva" petered out with a blip.

Quincy looked at the phone, and then at her, and thumped his tail as if he'd just given her the best present a dog could ever have dreamed up.

She sighed. "Elvis has left the building."

CECILIA PHONED MARJORIE from Jake's apartment. She walked in nervous circles, picking up knickknacks and examining photos en route.

Whatever she'd expected Jake's place to look like, this wasn't it.

It didn't resemble a cheesy bachelor pad or a dorm room in the least. Instead the small apartment was done in tasteful earth tones, and reflected Jake's affinity for earthiness, with woven hemp area rugs, oriental wall hangings and simple wood furniture.

It suited him well.

As she examined a small statue of Buddha, Marjorie answered her cell phone.

"It's Cecilia. I wondered if you'd be up for another party."

"Are you kidding? When?"

"Tomorrow night."

Marjorie whistled. "That's quick."

"I know. But something came up and I… I need to see everybody."

"Gotcha," Marjorie said.

"Think you can round up some friends for me? I hate to ask, but I'm sort of pressed for time."

"Honey, I'll have them beating down the door."

"Cover charges due by tomorrow morning, in my mail slot."

"That shouldn't be a problem."

"Thanks, Marjorie. I owe you big. I'll see you at the house tomorrow night, eight o'clock. Okay?"

Marjorie hesitated. "Will Devon be there?"

"I'll make sure he is."

Marjorie gave a little schoolgirlish squeal, completely at odds with her usual Mae-Westish temperament. "You're the best," she said, and hung up.

Jake emerged from the bedroom in a pair of khakis and a sea-green sweater that matched his eyes, his damp hair combed back from his forehead. He wrapped his arms around her waist, and she breathed in the woodsy scent of his cologne.

"Was that Marjorie?"

"Yes. She says she can line up some clients, no problem."

"Good. I'll drop you off at the office so you can call the caterer and the musicians, and I'll get to work on the guys."

Cecilia ran her fingers through his hair and kissed him. "By the way, Marjorie asked specifically for Devon."

Jake grinned. "They did seem to hit it off. Did you hear what they did in the pool house—?"

Cecilia covered her ears. "La-la-la-la-la. I don't want to hear about it. Bridge party, remember? I know nothing."

"Oh, right." Jake laughed. "Just tell the bartender to bring an extra jar of maraschino cherries. And remind the caterer to skip the shrimp puffs."

CHAPTER 20

*Working nights and weekends is a good thing. It means
you're busy.*

"Well, well. Look who's decided to grace us with her
presence." Beverly tossed a stack of contracts onto the
processor's desk as Cecilia walked through the door.

Cecilia looked at Beverly over the top of her sunglasses.
"I see the operation was unsuccessful."

"What operation?"

"The operation to remove the stick from your ass."

Beverly rolled her eyes. "Oh, you're just hilarious."

"Somebody's got to lighten the mood around here.
What's going on?"

"Steve wants to see you," the scheduler, Michael Floren-
tine, said from his desk near the front doors. "Right away."

Uh-oh.

Steve Belkin, the other half of Belkin-Frye, was rarely
in the office. And while Monty Frye had adored Cecilia,
Steve was less than enamored with her. Cecilia once heard
him describe her as a cobra with tits.

"Listen," Cecilia told Michael, "I lost my cell phone this morning, and I'm waiting to hear from an important client. His name's Nigel Lerwick. If he calls, put him right through to me, okay?"

"Will do."

She unloaded her stuff on her desk and headed straight for Steve's office, a firm believer in yanking out the bad tooth as soon as you feel the pain.

She knocked twice on the open door.

Steve swiveled his chair to face her. His hair, tastefully graying at the temples, was perfect as always. His chiseled good looks were the talk of every female client who walked through the door. They left Cecilia cold.

"Cecilia," Steve said, waving her in. "Close the door behind you, please."

She did as he said and took a seat in one of the stiff leather-and-chrome guest chairs against the wall. "I understand you wanted to see me?"

"I do." Steve leaned his elbows on his desk and tented his fingers beneath his chin. "We should talk."

"Of course. About anything specific?"

"Specifically about your performance as of late."

Oh, boy.

"Steve, I know I've been off my game a bit lately, but—"

He held up his hand to stop her, and picked up a sheet of paper from his desk. He perused it a moment before saying, "The year before last, you did thirty-five million in sales. Last year, forty-two million. This year to date? Seventeen million, and nothing since May. That's quite a gap."

"I know. I'm sorry. But the market hasn't been great."

"You know what we say around here. The *market* is where you buy groceries. We sell *real estate*. Real estate isn't a product, it's an emotional investment. If you can't convince people to make emotional investments, you have no business being in this business."

"I understand. But it's been a tough year in lots of ways."

Steve sighed. "I know Monty's death must have been difficult for you, and I know you're having some problems at home. But you have to move on. At this rate, you won't make it into the Platinum Club this year. You'll be lucky if you make the Pewter Club."

What could she say? A free trip to Hawaii wasn't exactly her priority now, anyway. "I'm sorry, Steve. I really am."

"You've borrowed twenty thousand dollars against your commissions, too." Steve lowered his voice. "And there's talk you may be having an affair with your *assistant*."

A shock wave ran through Cecilia's system. *"What?"*

Steve shook his head. "I don't have to tell you, that kind of thing can open us up to a messy lawsuit." He leaned back in his chair, giving her a Father-Knows-Best look. "It's grounds for dismissal. You know that, don't you?"

She nodded.

Steve straightened his tie, an indication that their little

meeting was wrapping up. "We'd like to see more of you around here. Starting today."

"Will do."

"Good. Now, you have a little more than a month to make some sales. Get out there and do it. Live up to your rep."

"Right. Absolutely."

When Cecilia opened the door, Beverly all but fell into the office.

"Could you hear okay?" Cecilia said.

"Hear what?" Beverly yawned, patting her mouth with hands that sported fierce-looking red claws. "I have some papers for Steve to sign."

"I'm sure." Cecilia stalked to her office and slammed the door.

She had no doubt who put a bug in Steve's ear about her and Jake. But the thing was, it wasn't a lie.

She *was* having an affair with her assistant, and it was unprofessional and dangerous and grounds for dismissal. But it was so much fun.

Despite what was happening with the car and the drugs and the parties, she was having *fun*. She wasn't the same tense, driven, obsessive woman she'd been just a few short weeks ago.

Monty would have been heartbroken.

He'd tried so hard to mold her. To teach her everything he knew.

For the sake of Monty's memory, she had to get her head back in the game. She had to end this silly fling with Jake. It had already dulled her edge, and now it was going to get her fired.

She picked up the picture of Brian from her desk, and traced the outline of his face with her fingertip.

What did she really think, anyway? That Jake was going to want to marry a forty-year-old woman with a ten-year-old son? That he would want an instant family, including a child with a learning disability and the responsibilities that went with it?

No, she wasn't about to let her life fall apart for a fling, no matter how much fun it might be. And she didn't have to have a man in her life.

She could do it all on her own.

"WHAT'S THE MATTER?" Jake said, as soon as he walked into her office.

"Nothing, why?"

"You're tense, and your aura is murky. I thought we took care of that this morning."

She almost smiled, but then remembered that she was ending things. Today. Now. "My aura is just fine, thanks."

Jake went to close the door to her office, but she stopped him. He gave her a questioning look, which she ignored.

She wasn't about to make Steve wonder what was going on behind a closed door.

"Everything good on your end?" Jake asked.

"Yes, the caterer and the bartenders and the music are all taken care of. What about you?"

"It's all good. Tomorrow night, eight o'clock. You talk to Nigel?"

"No. I tried calling his cell phone a few times, and left a message on his voice mail for him to call me at the office. I told Michael to put him right through to my phone if he calls. But I was in and out with a couple of clients, so I might have missed him.

"Meanwhile I have to get a new cell phone and get home to Quincy. He's probably eating the entire oven, piece by piece."

"I'll take you right now. And then maybe we can do something about that aura."

Cecilia sighed. "Jake, we have to talk."

"Uh-oh. That can't be good. I know that tone."

"Not here, okay?" She turned off her computer and gathered up her things. "Let's not leave together," she said in a low voice. "I'll meet you at your car."

"So what's up, Mata Hari?" Jake said, as she slid into the passenger seat. "Why can't we be seen leaving together all of a sudden?"

"Beverly told Steve we're having an affair."

"So what? It's her word against ours."

"He threatened to fire me."

Jake exhaled loudly. "What a jackass."

She shook her head. "He's well within his rights. The company has a no-fraternization policy. I know that. You know that. We screwed up."

"I'm sorry, but I can't look at it that way. What we did—what we're *doing*—isn't a mistake."

"Oh, no? Then what is it?"

Jake shrugged. "Fate, I guess."

If he hadn't been so serious, she might have laughed. "There's no such thing as fate."

"Karma, then. You're my reward for being a good person in a former life."

Now she did laugh. "I'm no prize, Jake. Just ask Ben."

"Ben didn't deserve you. Or Brian."

"Jake, stop. I'm telling you we can't keep going with this. For lots of reasons, not just Steve. It's been fun, but we've got to end it."

"That's all it was for you? Fun?"

What was she supposed to say? That he made her feel beautiful and sexy and young? That they were fantastic together? That he had somehow managed to pour himself into every part of her life, and fill in all the cracks and holes that she'd never managed to fix before he came along?

That she cared about him more than she ever thought possible?

It was all true. Impossibly true.

And impossible to admit.

It was a matter of self-preservation, really. She had to save her job and her sanity and her dignity.

"Yes, Jake. It was fun. But it *has* to end."

Jake let his head fall back against the headrest and closed his eyes for a few seconds. "All right. I'll make a deal with you."

"What's that?"

He turned and looked into her eyes. "If you can go until midnight tomorrow night without telling me you want me and you love me and you need me, I'll accept all of this. I'll go back to being just your assistant, no argument."

"No argument?"

"None. In fact, I will consider the window on our relationship closed completely. But if you *do* admit you love me, we quit Belkin-Frye and we see how far this thing can go. Deal?"

"You're talking to a woman who's made a life out of making deals, remember?"

Jake shook his head. "This isn't about real estate, Cecilia."

But it *was*. Because her heart was the most valuable real estate she owned. And she wasn't about to sell it to just anybody.

At THREE O'CLOCK in the morning, Cecilia gave up trying to sleep and went downstairs to the kitchen to make some tea, Quincy following close on her heels.

She could still smell a hint of Jake's cologne on the pillowcases, and she wasn't sure if she should wash them or put them in an airtight baggie to preserve the smell, so she could open the bag whenever she needed a Jake-fix.

Their dalliance had lasted less than seventy-two hours, and had been over for merely eight—if she were examined by a CSI team, his fingerprints would still be all over her body—but in that short time she'd become accustomed to thinking of him as more than her assistant.

This was crazy. Absolutely nuts. She was obsessing, and she knew it. If she had a car, she would have done a drive-by on his apartment. If she had a notebook, she would have written their names in bubble letters inside a big heart on the front of it.

Cecilia 'n' Jake.

"What am I going to do, Quincy?" she said, reaching down to scratch the dog's head. "I've got it bad."

Quincy stared up at her and thumped his tail on the Mexican tile.

When she'd come home the evening before, there had been a message from Dannie on the machine saying she would pick Quincy up on Wednesday morning. She was loath to admit it, but she was going to miss the big doofus.

There had been no message from Nigel, however.

She wondered if he'd been trying to call her cell phone. The salesclerk at the cell phone kiosk had refused to replace the phone Quincy had half digested until payment for Cecilia's last two bills was received.

Cecilia had tried several more times to get in touch with Nigel from home, but now his voice mail was full. She didn't like it, but she was just going to have to assume he could put Gordon off until tomorrow night.

She looked at her watch. Or rather, tonight.

She *had* to get some sleep. Being a madam was tiring, even when she was well rested.

IN THE MORNING, by the time Cecilia had come downstairs showered, dressed and dreading the day, a dozen envelopes of varying colors and sizes littered the floor beneath her mail slot, along with a note written in Marjorie's sprawling script: "Darling, hope these help. See you tonight. Love, M."

With her only fingernail that hadn't yet been chewed off, Cecilia opened the envelopes one by one, stacking by denomination the cash enclosed.

Three thousand dollars in each. The cover charges for the party.

More than enough to get her Cayenne out of hock.

The knot in her chest eased just a little. Things were going to be fine. Just fine.

Weren't they?

CHAPTER 21

Gordon Wiley despised cheap hotels, and he despised limey bastards who tried to screw him over.

He trudged up the stucco-and-cement stairwell of the Cozy Inn, which opened on each landing to a view of the parking lot below. When he reached the third floor, he rested for a moment against a wrought-iron railing, pulling a slip of paper from the pocket of his sheepskin jacket. He checked the number: 306.

Gordon followed the narrow balcony until he reached Limey's room, rapping hard on the door with his knuckles.

Not surprisingly, there was no answer.

Gordon pressed his ear to the door and could hear the television playing.

He stifled a yawn.

He shoulda sent Joey or Stretch, but he was a firm believer in doing his own dirty work. In fact, he sort of enjoyed it. It kept things real. Kept the fire burning.

Some guys, they made it to his level and they got soft. Started to think of themselves as businessmen rather than dealers. That was a mistake.

It was just like when Rocky Balboa went soft in *Rocky III*. Or was it *Rocky IV*? He could never remember. Anyway, Rocky turned into a suit and lost the eye of the tiger.

Gordon had no intention of losing the eye of the tiger. And it was stuff like this—teaching Limey respect—that was gonna help him keep it.

He cracked his neck, still thick and muscular after years of playing semipro football, and knocked on the door again, this time using his platinum-and-diamond pinky ring for extra effect.

"Yo, Limey. Let me in."

Nothing.

Gordon slid a crowbar out of his sleeve and pushed the wedge into the doorjamb near the lock. One quick jerk and the wood around the lock splintered. The door swung open.

The stench from inside hit Gordon like a physical thing, knocking him back over the threshold momentarily. He took a deep breath, covered his mouth and nose with the crook of his arm and went in.

The room was dark. An episode of *Laverne and Shirley* played on the television, which was attached with a bicycle chain to a stand that was bolted to the floor. The canned laughter from the show sounded tinny over the ancient set.

Gordon loved *Laverne and Shirley*. Especially when Lenny and Squiggy came on.

It took a moment for his eyes to adjust to the lack of light. When they did, he finally saw Nigel.

Tangled in a mess of sheets and blankets and puke lay the limey bastard, his body curled in a fetal position, pale and shaking. No wonder he hadn't been returning Gordon's calls.

He was totally strung out.

"Asshole," Gordon said. He'd been around enough to know that Nigel had been drinking heavily and had probably done enough heroin to kill a rhino.

Gordon closed the motel room door and hit the lights, pulling on a pair of latex gloves he'd taken from his pocket. He'd brought them so as not to get his hands bloody while he was beating Nigel to a pulp. If there was one thing he'd taken away from his miserable experience in the Boy Scouts—besides a shitload of mosquito bites—it was to always be prepared.

"You been a bad boy, Limey. Why haven't you called me?"

Nigel groaned and pulled the filthy sheets over his naked body.

Gordon raised him by the hair into a seated position. Nigel's eyes were large and very black. They reminded Gordon of the buttons on his grandmother's favorite sweater.

"Where's my blow, Nigel? You sell it to somebody else?"

Nigel's tongue lolled out of his mouth. "Nawww."

"Where is it then? 'Cause I got people waiting."

Nigel mumbled.

"What?" Gordon jerked Limey's head. "Speak up."

"Real estate lady. She told me to stall you."

"Real estate lady? What real estate lady?"

Nigel opened his mouth, and puked all over the bed.

"Jesus. That's freakin' disgusting." Gordon let go of Nigel's hair and he crumpled back onto the bed.

Gordon searched the drawers and cabinets in the motel room, but found no sign of his product. Not that he'd expected to. Nigel would have been lying there strung out on *cocaine* if he'd had it.

Never trust a doper.

With one finger, Gordon poked at the trash on the fabricated oak bedside table. Under a crumpled fast food wrapper, he found Nigel's cell phone. He flipped it open and scrolled through the recent calls.

Three in a row to "C. Katz."

Gordon pressed redial. It was answered immediately by voice mail.

"You've reached the cell phone of Cecilia Katz. I'm unavailable right now, but if you need immediate assistance, call my office…"

Gordon scrambled for a pen and scratched the phone number on a ketchup-stained napkin.

He pulled Nigel's head up again, and shoved the napkin beneath Limey's nose. "This the real estate lady you were talking about? Cecilia Katz?"

Nigel's head lolled.

"Was that a nod?"

His head lolled again.

"Good."

Gordon sat on the edge of the bed, careful to avoid the vomit, and dialed.

A woman with a voice like melted butter answered the phone.

"Belkin-Frye Real Estate."

"Yeah. Can I speak to Cecilia?"

The woman hesitated. "This wouldn't happen to be Nigel, would it?"

Bingo. "As a matter of fact, it would."

"Well, Mr. Lerwick, Cecilia isn't here at the moment. But she asked me to take care of you. I think I have exactly what you're looking for."

"You do, huh?"

The woman gave a breathy laugh. "Absolutely. You won't be disappointed."

"What's your name, sweetheart?"

"Beverly. Beverly Banff."

"Okay, Beverly. How do we get together?"

After making plans to meet with the real estate broad, Gordon stuffed the napkin and Nigel's phone in his pocket. Then he yanked the power cord of the little digital alarm clock out of the wall.

"Limey, I'm afraid we got some business to take care of."

When it was over, Gordon removed the latex gloves

with a snap, pulled the filthy sheets over a whimpering Nigel Lerwick, and went to the door.

He paused with his hand on the knob, and looked at the TV. Lenny and Squiggy were trying to join the circus.

Gordon snickered.

He loved that show.

CHAPTER 22

Your job, in a nutshell, is to know your clients' needs.

Hanging around the office all day sucked.

Cecilia toyed with her coffee mug, debating the merits of a fourth cup. She was already wound pretty tight, but she was afraid she'd fall asleep at her desk and miss Nigel's call.

Jake had come by her house that morning to drive her to the bank, where she'd paid the deficiency on her Cayenne. Now all she had to do was wait for the paperwork to go through, and pray no one looked in the spare-tire well before the car was released to her sometime this afternoon.

In the interim, she had to put in her time at the office, per Steve's directive.

So she stared at the phone, checked her e-mail for the fifteenth time, fantasized about cigarettes, fantasized about Jake and tapped out an SOS message in Morse code with her stapler.

Screw it. A fourth cup of coffee sounded perfect.

As she passed through the main office, Beverly was

hunched over the phone, murmuring. She hung up as Cecilia walked by.

"Was that your plastic surgeon, Bev? I understand ear-lobe liposuction is big these days. You'd better hurry up and get some."

Bev gave her a sweet smile. "Too bad you haven't tried it. Those earrings are looking a little snug."

Cecilia picked up a photograph of Beverly's cats dressed in prairie bonnets and aprons. "What darling children. They look just like you." She set the picture down, leaned over Bev's desk and whispered, "That wasn't a call from one of my clients, was it?"

Bev's smile disappeared. "I'm getting tired of your nasty accusations."

"Nasty but true. I'd watch my back if I were you."

"And I'd shave my eyebrows if I were *you*," Bev called after Cecilia, who was already halfway to the kitchen.

By five, Cecilia was completely strung out on caffeine.

She'd filed two new listings, cleaned out her desk, re-designed her newsletter, color coded her files and made out her Christmas shopping list, which was a good deal shorter than it had been the year before. Partly because she no longer had a husband, but mostly because she no longer had money.

The office was quiet for a Tuesday afternoon. Even Beverly had taken off for Mayor Sundberg's rally, so Cecilia couldn't even pass the time trading barbs.

When Jake finally walked into her office, she sprang out of her chair like a jack-in-the-box.

"Oh, thank God. I'm going crazy here. Nigel still hasn't called, and his voice mail is still full. I'm starting to get worried. Do you think I should call Don?"

Jake whistled through his teeth. "How many cups of coffee have you had?"

"Five. No, six. I think. Why?"

"No reason. Are you ready to go pick up your car? I'll drive you to the repo lot. Then I'm going to head over to the Grove place and get things started."

"Right. Sure. The party. You bet." She shrugged into her coat and grabbed her purse. "Well, come on. What are you waiting for?"

Jake shook his head and followed her out.

At the repo lot a receptionist with hair the color of blue cotton candy directed them to a waiting area while Cecilia's car was brought around.

Cecilia paced the small perimeter of the room while Jake flipped through the channels of a television in the corner.

"Who watches *Laverne and Shirley* anymore?" he said.

"How can you watch TV at a time like this?"

"It's a unique ability passed on through the Y chromosome."

"Like the ability to pee standing up?"

"Uh-oh," Jake said.

Cecilia stopped pacing. "What?"

"Look."

Nigel's bloated face appeared in a small box above a news anchorman's head, with the words "Nigel Lerwick, Drummer" beneath.

Cecilia ran to the TV. "Turn it up! Hurry!"

"…police were called late this afternoon to the Cozy Inn Motel, after a maid discovered a body in one of the rooms. Nigel Lerwick, former drummer for the Aching Loins, a popular rock group in the nineteen eighties, was found dead from an apparent drug overdose. In other news…"

Cecilia's racing heart skittered to a stop. "Oh, no. Oh, my God. What are we going to do?"

Jake switched off the television set and came to her, just in time. Her knees gave way and he caught her, holding her tight against him until the shaking stopped.

"What are we going to do?" she repeated.

Jake sat her down on one of the orange molded-plastic chairs. "We're going to get your car and make sure what we need is still there. And then we're going to call Don Grove and figure out how the hell to get out of this mess."

BACK AT HER PLACE, Cecilia hung up the phone. "No answer. Now what?"

Jake shook his head. "The party starts in an hour. We've got to get over there. I don't know what we *can* do right now."

Cecilia was beyond needing a cigarette. She needed a bottle of Wild Turkey, a long vacation and possibly some heavy sedatives.

"I'll tell you what we're going to do," she said. "When we get through this party—*if* we get through this party—we're going to put that cocaine back in Candy's closet with the Jimmy Choos and get the hell out of that house. For good. Let Don figure out how to get rid of it."

"The cocaine or the house?"

"Both."

"I think that's a wise decision."

Cecilia was dying for Jake to put his arms around her and tell her everything was going to be okay. But of course he didn't. And he wouldn't.

He was waiting for her to confess her undying love.

And she wouldn't. She could make it another five and a half hours without breaking down. She could!

By midnight tonight she would have proven to Jake and, more importantly, to herself that she didn't need a man to survive.

"I guess we should get going," Jake said, helping her on with her coat. His fingertips brushed her bare shoulders, and she gave an involuntary shiver.

Quincy followed them to the door, his tongue lolling out of his mouth, his eyes mournful.

"Can we take him?"

Jake sounded like a ten-year-old who'd just found a stray.

"No way. You know how he is. He'll just get into trouble."

Quincy cocked his head and gave a little whine.

"But he's been alone all day," Jake said. "Is that really the way we should treat the dog who saved my life?"

Quincy yipped, which Cecilia would have sworn sounded exactly like, "Right! Right!"

She rolled her eyes. "Okay. But he has to stay in the garage."

"Don't worry. He'll be a good boy."

"I wouldn't put money on that one."

When they got to the Grove house, the caterer's truck was waiting in the drive.

Cecilia unlocked the house and let them in, and she and Jake readied the house, starting the fireplaces, putting on music and turning on lights.

Half an hour later, the boys filed in. They looked as yummy as they had before, but something was different. *Someone* was different.

"Who are we missing?" she said.

"Ahmed and Dave couldn't make it tonight," Chuck answered. "These guys are replacements."

"Don't I know you two from somewhere?" Cecilia said.

"Yes, ma'am," said one of the new guys. "I mean, Yes, miss."

Cecilia narrowed her eyes. "Aren't you the bag boys from my supermarket?"

"He's a bag boy. I'm actually a checker," said the other. "And you're the lady who made us look at her butt."

Cecilia felt faint. "Jake...?"

"We needed the extra bodies, so to speak."

"I recommended them," Chuck said. "They're in my frat."

Oh, wonderful.

"I don't know about this," she said. They were certainly good-looking enough, but neither one seemed terribly bright.

Jake pulled her aside. "Our boys were wiped out by the end of the night last time. Imagine if there were two fewer tonight."

"I understand. But—"

"Hey, don't worry. It'll be okay. Besides, the women will be here any minute."

CHAPTER 23

A blonde in a red Maserati pulled up in front of Gordon's hotel.

Gorgeous. And the broad wasn't bad, either.

Gordon checked his watch. Right on time.

The woman got out of the car, spoke briefly with the bellhop and then strolled into the lobby like she owned the place.

"You Beverly?" he said as she passed him.

She stopped and turned around. "Mr. Lerwick?"

"Right. That's me. Call me Nigel."

For a minute Gordon worried that she might have seen the news. He hadn't actually meant for Limey to die, but he supposed the trauma of the beating was exacerbated by the drugs. Lerwick didn't look too healthy to begin with. No great loss.

Beverly extended a manicured hand and he grasped it, glad that he'd taken the time to come back to his hotel to change before meeting her.

Maybe when they'd finished taking care of business, they could move on to some pleasure.

"It's so nice to meet you, Nigel. I'm sorry to have had to

do this so late, but I had a commitment I couldn't get out of. Lucky for me, the guest of honor came down with food poisoning, and the event was cut short."

"Hey, no problem."

"I'm parked right out front. We can take my car, or yours if you prefer."

"Let's take yours. It's a beauty." He held the lobby door open for her. "Hey, you mind if I drive?"

"Whatever makes you happy." She gave him a killer smile and dropped the car keys into the palm of his hand.

He opened the passenger-side door for her and then ran around the car and eased his stocky frame into the driver's seat. "Nice. I drive a Rolls Corniche myself, but my first luxury car was a Maserati."

He fired up the engine and pulled out of the hotel's parking circle and onto a two-lane highway.

"A Corniche, eh?" Beverly slid a little closer. "I bought this one used, and I'll have to skip lunch and dinner for two years to afford it. Unless, of course, you decide to buy something from me." She laughed.

"Don't see why I wouldn't. So where we going?"

"Not far. Make a right at the second light."

Gordon pressed ever so lightly on the gas pedal, and the car leaped like a Thoroughbred jumping a fence.

Beverly laughed again and slid so close to him that her tit pressed against his arm.

Gordon smiled.

Oh, yeah. He couldn't wait to get done with business.

They drove for a few minutes in silence, Gordon testing the power of the car and sneaking peeks at blondie's long legs and short skirt.

"This is it. Turn here."

Gordon guided the Maserati onto a long, tree-lined drive, to a home that looked like something out of a movie. Sculpted hedges framed a boxy, three-story brick house with white gables and cornices.

"This your place?" Gordon said.

"It's mine." Beverly opened the car door and swung her legs out, baring the tops of thighs that looked better than vanilla ice cream.

Gordon followed her up the walkway to the front door, where she opened a lockbox on the knob.

"You selling it?" he said.

She gave him a strange look. "Of course."

She opened the door and ushered him inside, turning on a light switch to illuminate a wide hall with parquet floors and a two-story ceiling. Above them, a teardrop chandelier cast fractured light onto the walls.

"What do you think?" she said.

He nodded. "Nice."

She gave him the thousand-watt smile. "What would you like to see first? The master bedroom, maybe?"

Gordon grinned. "You're a fast worker, huh?"

She touched his arm. "Well, I don't believe in wasting

time. But if you'd prefer to take things more slowly, we can start in the kitchen."

"What I'd prefer is to take care of business first, and then we can go look at the bedroom."

"Of course."

Gordon followed Beverly through the house as she turned on lights and fluffed pillows.

"The place doesn't have to look perfect," he said. "I just want my stuff."

"Your stuff? What stuff?"

Gordon got a bad feeling. "The stuff you said you had for me."

Beverly stopped smiling. "I'm sorry. I don't understand. I thought you wanted to look at houses."

Gordon's mood went black. "Why the f—" He took a deep breath and dragged a hand through his hair. "Why would I want to look at *houses?*"

"I thought… Weren't you going to look at houses with Cecilia?"

Gordon shook his head.

"Then what were you going to do?"

"You're kidding me, right? You told me she wanted you to take care of me."

Beverly took a subtle step back. "Yes, but…"

"So what the hell is this? Is she screwing me over or what?"

"I…no. No, she's not screwing you over." She touched his arm and then pulled her hand away as if it had been burned. "To tell you the truth, I think this whole thing is a big misunderstanding."

"A misunderstanding."

"Right. You see, I was on floor time when you called—that's when one agent takes the calls for the whole office—and I thought you were one of Cecilia's clients."

Like a frog catching a spider, Gordon reached out and pulled Beverly up against him, covering her mouth with his hand. "Shut up."

She nodded, her china-blue eyes wide with shock.

"Are you a cop?"

She shook her head.

"You sure you're not a cop?"

She shook her head again.

"Good. Listen up. I don't want a big song and dance. I want my cocaine, and I want it now. Do you have it?"

She shook her head.

"Do you know where it is?"

Again she shook her head.

"Do you know where Cecilia is?"

Her eyes grew bigger. He released his hand from her mouth so she could speak, but continued to hold her elbow in a viselike grip.

"She was still at the office when I left."

Gordon pulled Nigel's phone out of his pocket and hit redial then shoved the phone at Beverly. "Ask for her. And don't try anything, or I'll break your arms."

She nodded.

"Hi, Michael, it's Beverly. Is Cecilia still in? Oh. Okay, thanks. No, I'll find her."

Gordon took the phone away from her ear.

"She left over an hour ago," Beverly said. She looked like she might cry.

"You know her cell number?"

Beverly shook her head. "It doesn't matter anyway. She lost her cell phone this morning."

Gordon handed Beverly the phone again. "Find her."

CHAPTER 24

Contacts are a real estate agent's currency.

Marjorie was the first of the women to arrive, and immediately located Devon—by the food, of course.

Five of the other guests were repeat customers, two or three Cecilia recognized from the society pages—Marjorie had some very influential friends—and a couple she knew from her spinning class. She wondered if it would be awkward running into them at the gym on Saturday.

The women and men quickly paired off, disappearing and reappearing as the night wore on.

Cecilia mingled and made introductions and replenished drinks, all the while watching the clock. And watching Jake.

She thought about all the little things he'd done for her, not only during their brief affair but over the entire time she'd known him.

Like once when he'd brought her a daisy in a paper cup to brighten up her office. Or all the Saturdays he hung out at her place with Brian when Ben was golfing and she had a house to show. Or the times he'd stayed late at the office with her while she finished up paperwork, so she wouldn't have to be alone.

He'd cooked her dinners, nursed her through hangovers and brought her soup when she was sick. Jake had always been a good friend as well as a fabulous assistant.

And when they'd finally become lovers, the way he touched her and kissed her and made her feel like the center of the universe...well, that didn't suck, either.

She looked around at the women at the party, laughing and flirting with all the gorgeous men, sparkling more brightly than all the jewels they wore. If they were feeling one-tenth of what she'd felt with Jake, then this party was a good thing.

Every woman who'd ever mourned the loss of her sex appeal, who'd ever entertained the notion that she could no longer be attractive to the opposite sex, should have the right to get laid by an adoring mimbo at least once in her life, just to replenish the waters in her well of self-esteem.

Maybe more than once, she thought, as she caught Marjorie and Devon going off together for the third time.

Cecilia checked her watch.

Nine-thirty.

She cast a glance in Jake's direction. He smiled, as if he'd been waiting for her to look his way.

She busied herself rearranging the crackers around a bowl of paté.

Just two and a half more hours...

Jake's cell phone rang, and out of the corner of her eye she could see him coming her way.

He handed her the ringing phone. "Look at the caller."

Cecilia read the LED screen. "Nigel's phone?" A chill ran over her, but she shook it off. It wasn't as if Nigel was reaching out from beyond.

"You going to answer it?" Jake asked.

Cecilia stared at the phone for a moment before flipping it open. "Hello?"

"Cecilia. I found you."

"Beverly? What are you doing with Nigel Lerwick's phone?"

"I don't—"

Beverly's voice cut out, replaced by a man's. "Who is this?"

"Who is *this*?"

A mirthless chuckle. "Take a wild guess."

"Gordon?"

"Give the lady a prize. Is this Cecilia Katz?"

Cecilia's heart thumped painfully. "Yes."

"You've got something of mine."

"Yes, I do."

"I want it."

"Yes, I know. And believe me, I want to give it to you."

"Good. Then we have something in common."

Jake looked at Cecilia expectantly, and she nodded.

"Where should we meet?" she said.

"You have the stuff with you?"

"Yes."

"Then I'll come to you.".

"That might not be the best idea—"

"It's the only idea." Gordon exhaled loudly. "First Nigel makes me hunt him down, and then you send me your little blond bitch."

"My blond bitch? I didn't—"

"Hey. Shut up. I'm done screwing around. You have the stuff? Then I'm coming to you."

Cecilia took a quick breath. "Okay. Absolutely." She gave him directions to Don's house and said, "There's a path off the driveway in front of the garage. Come around to the side door."

"I'll be there in a few minutes."

"Right. Good. Thanks."

Gordon hung up, and Cecilia handed Jake the phone back with trembling hands. "He's on his way. And for some reason he's with Beverly."

"Beverly? How would she have gotten in the middle of all this?"

They were silent for a moment, then Jake said, "Maybe she caught his call at the office."

"Oh, no. Oh, my God. She has no idea how dangerous he can be."

"Let's just hope she doesn't do anything to piss him off."

She and Jake looked at each other as if they were having the same thought.

Beverly pissed everyone off.

"She's as good as dead," Cecilia said softly.

Jake hugged her, and she pressed her face against the lapel of his suit, inhaling his Zenlike calm. Her nervousness gradually subsided, replaced by a numb sense of purpose.

"Make sure everything runs smoothly," she said. "I'm going to wait by the side door for Gordon."

Jake looked as if he wanted to argue, but instead he said, "Keep Quincy with you, okay?"

"Will do."

She located her handbag, found her keys and opened the door to the garage. Quincy lay on a pile of old carpet, chewing the rim from a bike tire. When he saw her come in, he wagged his entire body.

"Hi, buddy. You want to go outside?"

Quincy yipped, and Cecilia pressed the automatic garage door button, careful to take a wide berth around Don Grove's vintage Austin Healy as she walked Quincy out.

She opened the rear hatch to the Cayenne and Quincy jumped in, scrambling over the back seats and into the passenger side, thumping his tail expectantly.

"We're not going anywhere right now," she said. "Come on out of there."

Quincy wouldn't budge. He wanted to go for a ride.

Cecilia cajoled and pleaded and made kissy noises, but the dog refused to come out.

"Fine. Stay there, then."

Just as she was about to pull up the carpet to get to the spare-tire well, headlights flashed on the lonely country road leading to the Groves' driveway.

Wow. Gordon was quick.

She squinted into the dark. What she saw made her insides go liquid.

It wasn't Gordon coming up the drive after all. It was a police cruiser. Or rather, a slew of police cruisers.

She slammed the hatch of the Cayenne shut just as the first cop car pulled up to her, nearly trapping her between the vehicles.

The officer got out of the car. "Evening, Ms. Katz."

"Good evening, Chief. Are you here to harass me again?"

"Actually, ma'am, I'm not. I'm here to arrest you."

Cecilia locked her knees so they wouldn't fold. "Excuse me?"

Three other police cars pulled up behind Chief McAllister's. Cops poured out. McAllister directed them to stay put. He moved in and took Cecilia's elbow. "I'm here to arrest you."

"For what?"

"Pandering."

"Pandering?"

"Procuring prostitutes."

"That's insane—"

McAllister pulled her out from between the cars. "Put your palms on the vehicle and spread your legs."

"Absolutely not. I have a brokers' tour going on inside, and I'm going back in there."

"Another brokers' tour? Fine. If that's the way you want to play it." McAllister grabbed her elbow, steering her toward the house. "We'll do this inside."

He motioned to the other officers. Four of them went around the back of the house, while two others went to the front door. McAllister and another cop escorted Cecilia through the open garage door.

McAllister's gun belt scraped along the side of the Austin Healy.

"Chief McAllister, can't we discuss this?"

"Nope. I got two young men who were bragging to their friends that they were going to be paid for sex here tonight. Suddenly everything made sense to me. Why all the older women and younger men."

They entered the house through the laundry room door. Already the place was chaos. Cops rousted half-dressed men and women from every room in the house, herding them into the great room.

McAllister cuffed Cecilia's hands in front of her, and she stood near one of the big stone fireplaces, watching her world fall apart .

She searched frantically for Jake, who finally was led in handcuffs into the room, speaking calmly with the officer who escorted him. He caught Cecilia's gaze and held it, and she imagined he was projecting positive energy her way.

It wasn't working.

There was absolutely nothing positive about the situation. That is, until Marjorie appeared.

She and Devon were brought in by a short, red-haired, freckled officer who looked as if he'd just graduated from middle school. Marjorie was in her bra and skirt. Devon sported a pair of red boxer shorts that said Ride the Pipe on the seat.

Hadn't Jake taught him anything?

Marjorie didn't look the least bit cowed, despite her state of undress. In fact, she looked angry.

She spied Chief McAllister from across the room and marched over, making the plastic zip-strip that served as handcuffs look like an accessory rather than a detention device.

"Avery, what is the meaning of all this?"

Chief McAllister removed his hat. His face was red, all the way up to his bald spot. "Mrs. Almswhite. What are you doing here?"

Cecilia could tell he was trying not to look at Marjorie's bra.

"I'm attending a party, of course," Marjorie said. "Having a wonderful time. At least I was, until you and your friends arrived."

"You shouldn't be here, Mrs. Almswhite." The chief spoke in a low voice, almost inaudible in the fray. "I'm going to take your cuffs off, and you go get dressed and get out of here."

"I will not. But I will allow you to remove this ridiculous plastic thing. Now, what is going on?'"

Chief McAllister shook his head but said, "This is a raid. We're arresting everyone here under suspicion of illegal activity."

"Are parties illegal now, Chief?"

"Of course not." If possible, the chief turned even redder. "But we have reports, and apparently evidence, of prostitution…" McAllister nodded in the direction of an officer who was carrying Jake's shoebox full of money up from the makeshift office in the basement.

Marjorie leaned in close. "Look around you, Chief. Do you see any familiar faces?"

McAllister scanned the room.

"Over there, by the window," Marjorie said. "That's Dori Campbell, Senator Campbell's ex-wife. And there, by the bronze sculpture of Elvis? Lisa Beales, the senator's most strident supporter and organizer of most of his fund-raisers."

McAllister shook his head. "We have six witnesses from the Grocery King who will swear that two of the men here were recruited for prostitution."

"Look. Coming down the steps," Marjorie said.

McAllister's jaw dropped. "That's Mayor Sundberg's *wife*. No wonder she wasn't at the rally tonight."

Marjorie nodded. "Aside from what this means to all of us personally, what do you think would happen if the media got wind of this? Elections are a week away."

McAllister was silent.

"Lives would be ruined, Chief McAllister. Yours and mine among them. And I'm not just saying this to save my own ass. Heaven knows I don't care what anyone thinks of me, but you've got two kids to put through college. What happens if you lose your reappointment?"

McAllister rubbed the back of his neck and looked at Cecilia. She raised her eyebrows hopefully.

"Listen to me, Avery," Marjorie said. "There's nothing illegal going on here. It's just a party."

"I can't explain this away," McAllister said.

"Sure you can. You tell whoever needs to know that it was all a mistake. A rumor. You investigated and found nothing."

Chief McAllister clenched his jaw but nodded.

Marjorie patted his shoulder. "Thank you, Avery. I won't forget this."

McAllister unlocked Cecilia's cuffs and gave her a look like the kid at Christmas who didn't get his favorite toy.

"Hold on, men," he shouted over the din. "We got some bad information."

When McAllister had walked away, Cecilia said, "Thank you, Marjorie. I owe you so big. If there's anything I can do for you, just let me know." She grabbed her friend and hugged her.

"We'll talk when this is all straightened out." Marjorie waggled her eyebrows.

Cecilia fought her way through the chaos to Jake's side. "We've got to call Nigel's phone," she whispered. "Tell Gordon not to come."

"If he hasn't already been here," Jake said.

"Let's hope not."

CHAPTER 25

Nigel's phone vibrated in Gordon's jacket pocket. He pulled it out, checked the number and flipped it open. "You trying to set me up?"

The Katz bitch whispered into the phone. "No! No. Absolutely not. We just ran into a snag."

"That's what you call a half-dozen cops swarming our meeting place? A snag?"

"They weren't here about...*that*. They were here for a different reason."

Gordon whistled into the phone. "You got problems, don't you, lady?"

"It's okay. Everything is fine. Just tell me where you are."

"Why? So you can have your friends come for a visit? No, thanks."

He could hear her breathing quicken. He liked that.

"Listen, I told you. The police had nothing to do with you or our arrangement. I have what you want, and I just want to get rid of it."

"Right."

Gordon had broken in to the Katz bitch's house and was

tossing his way through it as he talked, dragging Beverly by her skinny wrist and wondering where in the hell all the furniture was.

Nothing to search but a sideboard in the dining room and the kitchen cabinets. Except for a couple of ashtrays and a dumpy grandfather clock in the hall, there was nothing there.

"Just, please, tell me what to do," Cecilia said on the other end.

A litany of rude replies ran through Gordon's head, but he decided to be civil. For now, at least.

"Sit tight. I'll let you know. But first I gotta figure out how to make sure you won't screw me."

He closed the phone and stuck it back into his pocket.

He had blondie, but he'd gathered from their conversations that she and the Katz bitch weren't exactly best friends. The Katz bitch might not even care if Beverly suffered physical harm.

No, he needed something else. Something better.

"What am I looking for?" he muttered to himself.

"Can't you just let me go?" Beverly said, in what he imagined was her reasonable-real-estate-agent voice. "I told you, I don't have anything to do with this. I don't even *like* Cecilia."

"Funny how you ended up doing her dirty work."

"I *wasn't*. I thought you were a client. A *real estate* client. I was trying to *steal* you."

"Didn't anyone ever tell you stealing is wrong?" He dragged Beverly into the living room, also devoid of furniture.

"She moving?" he asked.

"Not that I know of."

Gordon spotted something lying on the floor in the corner. He went over and picked it up.

"Who's this?" He showed Beverly the picture of a kid in a sweatshirt.

"Her son, I guess."

"You guess?"

"I never saw him."

"Where is he?"

Beverly shrugged. "He goes to some boarding school."

"Where? Nearby?"

"I think so. Can we please get out of here?"

"In a minute."

Gordon plowed through the house with Beverly in tow, looking for something, though he wasn't sure what.

He found it, in the form of an envelope tacked to a bulletin board beside the phone in the kitchen.

"Bingo." He tucked the envelope into his coat and zipped it up.

"What's that?" Beverly asked.

Gordon pushed her toward the front door. "My insurance policy."

"HE'S AT MY HOUSE," Cecilia said, grabbing her purse and running for the door. "Let's go."

Jake was two steps behind her. "How do you know he's at your house?"

"Because I heard the grandfather clock chiming in the background when he called."

The police cars were still blocking the drive, so Cecilia drove across the yard, narrowly missing a fountain shaped like a giant fish head.

"Has off-roading been a lifelong hobby of yours, or is it something new?" Jake said.

"Hey, what's the point of having an SUV if you're not going to test it a little?"

They bumped onto the road and heard a yip from the back seat.

Quincy stuck his head between the seats.

"Jesus, he scared me," Cecilia said. "I forgot he was in here."

Quincy licked Cecilia's ear and flopped back down between the rows of seats.

Leave it to Quincy to nap at a time like this. That dog could sleep through anything.

"Listen, I don't want to throw a wrench into the works," Jake said, "but what are we going to do when we get to your place? I mean, the guy can obviously be dangerous. We can't just walk in there without protection."

"Good point." Cecilia drummed on the steering wheel, thinking.

"I should have some pepper spray in the glove compartment. And there's a pair of handcuffs under your seat."

"Handcuffs?" Clearly he though she was joking.

"Just look under the seat."

Jake switched on the map light over the dashboard and dug around under his seat, coming up with a small pink shopping bag.

"Open it," Cecilia said.

He pulled out a wad of tissue paper and unwrapped a pair of handcuffs covered in pink fur.

She could practically hear the gears turning in his mind.

"Relax. They aren't mine. I mean, I didn't buy them for myself."

"Mmm-hmm."

"They're not! I was going to put them in Beverly's purse the next time I knew she was taking a big client out to lunch. You know how she always has to pull everything out of that giant handbag to find her wallet."

"Good one."

"I know." Cecilia swallowed the lump forming in her throat. "I just hope Gordon doesn't do anything to hurt her. She's not my favorite person, but…"

"I know." Jake reached over and squeezed her hand. "Hey. We have the cocaine. And Quincy, too, if we need him."

At the mention of his name, the dog pushed his big head into the front again.

"How can we lose?" Cecilia said, her sarcasm completely lost on both Jake and Quincy.

They arrived at Cecilia's house a few minutes later, armed and dangerous. Or at least armed and capable of causing discomfort.

"I don't see anything," Cecilia said. There was no car in the drive, no lights on in the house.

"I doubt he'd be opening the door for us," Jake said.

"Should we split up or go in together?"

"I think we should stick together. There's safety in numbers."

"True. With Quincy, we'll just about look like the cavalry coming in."

Quincy snorted.

"Good horse impression," Jake said, patting him.

They grabbed the paper bag out of the spare tire well and went in through the front door, Cecilia pointing the Mace like a gun. "Hey. Gordon. Get in here."

No indication he was still in the house. But he had been.

The few pieces of furniture remaining had clearly been rifled through. In the dining room, table linens littered the floor. Upstairs her clothes were strewn into every corner.

Even the cabinet of the old grandfather clock in the hall stood open.

"I wonder where he went," Jake said, following Cecilia into the kitchen.

"I don't know. But he has to call soon." Cecilia picked

up the picture of Brian from the kitchen counter. "This isn't where I left it," she said. Her gaze moved around the kitchen, coming to rest on the bulletin board beside the phone. The envelope containing Brian's midterm grades—and the Catalina School's address—was gone.

"Oh, God. Jake. He's gone after Brian."

CHAPTER 26

"Where are we going?"

The blonde was starting to get on Gordon's nerves. He should have just shot her and dumped her somewhere, but it would have been a waste of a really fine piece of ass.

"You'll know when we get there," he said. He pressed the gas pedal, and the car responded. For a few minutes Gordon paid attention to nothing but the car and the winding back roads of southeastern Pennsylvania.

He couldn't wait to get back to New York.

Trees and wildlife brought back bad memories of camping trips with his father, who thought eating fish they'd caught for breakfast was a big freakin' treat. His father had loved all that outdoorsman crap.

Gordon, meanwhile, would have preferred watching a few Saturday-morning cartoons while having lox and bagels from the Second Avenue Deli.

"Where are you taking me?" Beverly said.

"I told you, you'll know when we get there."

"Are you going to hurt me?"

Her voice sounded funny. He tried to look over at her, to

get a read, but he had to concentrate on the curves in the road.

"What do you think?" he said. "You think I'm gonna hurt you?"

"Why are we turning onto Skippack Pike?"

"Because that's where the GPS is telling me to go."

"Onto *Skippack Pike?*"

She said it slowly, almost like she was dictating something—

Faster than a snake striking, Gordon reached over Beverly's lap and grabbed her wrist. She held a cell phone in her right hand, which she'd hidden against her thigh. The connection was open.

"Hello?" he said into the phone.

"This is the 911 operator," a voice intoned.

"Shit." He rolled down the window and threw the phone out into the darkness. "That wasn't nice."

Beverly wedged herself up against the car door as they sped along in inky darkness, broken only by an occasional passing car or lonely porch light.

"Where'd you get the phone?" he said, his tone menacingly conversational. He'd already confiscated the Black-Berry she wore clipped to her hip.

Beverly started crying. "I keep an extra in the glove compartment, just in case."

"You're just Little Miss Organized, aren't you?"

Gordon drove fast, turning off Skippack Pike and

getting mired in a maze of narrow roads and lanes, the voice on the GPS system repeatedly urging him to "turn around when possible."

He pulled over into an access lane beside a cornfield and killed the engine.

The blonde was breathing hard. She pawed at the door handle, trying to find the unlock button, but he was too quick for her. He grabbed her by the hair and hauled her over the center console, her high heels scraping the Maserati's sculpted leather dash as he dragged her out of the car.

He set her upright, and the heels of her shoes sank in the soft dirt.

Gordon reached into the back of his waistband for his gun, pressing the barrel to the underside of her chin. "That was a really stupid move, blondie."

"I know. I'm sorry. I'm just scared."

"Have I given you reason to be scared? Any reason at all?"

She shook her head.

"Then why'd you hafta do that?"

"I don't know. Really, I'm sorry." She sank to her knees, muddying the hem of her suit jacket.

Gordon made a sound like a deflating balloon. "So, what do you think we should do about this?"

CHAPTER 27

Keep the deal together no matter what you have to do.

"We're never going to catch up with him," Cecilia said as they flew over the dark back roads to Brian's school.

"Yes, we will," Jake said.

"He's got a twenty-minute lead on us, at least."

"We'll get him."

"What if he gets to Brian first?"

"He won't. They must have great security at the school. Even if Gordon makes it there before us, he'll never get into the dorm."

Cecilia exhaled loudly. "Do you always have to be so optimistic?"

"Do you always have to be so negative?"

"I'm not negative. I'm realistic."

"You're cynical, just like Monty was."

"I'm not cynical, I'm practical."

"How is negativity practical? You spend your whole life limiting yourself and others."

"I do not!"

"Yes, you do."

Cecilia gave a shout of frustration. "How? How do I limit people? I don't even understand that comment."

"Here's an example. You won't give me a chance, because you have some crazy, convoluted notion that people will react badly. You're limiting me, and you're limiting others."

"That's called realism, not negativity. And I don't want to talk about *us* right now. I'm dealing with a crisis."

"Okay, we won't talk about *us*. We'll talk about *you*, and how *you* limit yourself."

"Stop it."

"Why don't you believe you're capable of helping Brian?"

"Because I'm not. I'm not a therapist or a doctor or an educator."

"No, but you're his mother."

Cecilia gave a humorless laugh. "Anyone can be a mother, Jake. No qualifications necessary."

She turned onto Skippack Pike. Just five more minutes.

"True," Jake said. "Anyone can be a mother. But not everyone can be a *good* mother. That takes time and effort and sacrifice."

"Are you suggesting I don't sacrifice for my son?" She dragged a hand through her hair. "How do you think all of *this* started?"

"Because you're scared. Because doing this was easier than

bringing Brian home and putting yourself in a position to fail."

"I never should have told you what I told you in that repo yard."

"Why? Because you actually admitted you have feelings?"

"You're just mad because I don't have feelings for *you*."

Jake didn't seem the least bit upset by her words. "I don't believe that. And I don't think *you* do, either." He looked at his watch. "And you still have thirty-one minutes to admit it."

"You really are out of your mind."

"No, I'm not. I'm the best thing that ever happened to you besides your son, and you're too stubborn to admit it."

She didn't even argue. In part, because she knew he was just trying to distract her from freaking out about Brian, but also because she knew he was right. There was no one she would rather have had sitting beside her that moment.

Jake Eamon was the only person in the world she could count on. Even if his pie-eyed positivity had occasionally made the situation worse.

They flew past cow pastures and roadside antique shops, running through red lights and stop signs, not talking until they reached the turn onto the Catalina School campus.

"I hope we catch up to him before it's too late," she said quietly.

He put his hand on her shoulder. "We will."

For once, his optimism didn't make her crazy.

Cecilia drove as fast as she dared on the narrow, winding, tree-lined lane. Headlights flashed halfway up the hill, and she squinted into the night.

"That's Beverly's Maserati!"

"He's almost to the dorm," Jake said. "Hurry!"

"Hold on."

Cecilia found a break in the trees and swerved off the road onto the wide grass lawn.

"What are you doing?"

"Taking a more direct route."

She gunned the engine, speeding toward the hillside garden adjacent to the dorm.

"You're kidding, right?" Jake said. "We'll never make it up there this way."

"Now who's being negative?"

"I'm serious, Cecilia. If we get stuck, it's over."

"We won't get stuck," she said, with more confidence than she felt. "The Cayenne can traverse terrain at up to a forty-five-degree angle. At least, that's what the owner's manual says. I guess we'll see, won't we?"

They thumped over a shallow ditch that ran around the perimeter of the garden, forcing the nose of the Cayenne into the air like a jet taking off from a runway.

The rear wheels dug into the soft earth, spinning helplessly. For one terrifying moment, Cecilia thought she'd taken a gamble and lost.

But then the front tires gripped and the SUV leaped forward, churning up rosebushes and shrubbery and narrow gravel paths. She swerved to avoid a replica of the *Venus de Milo*, only to find herself driving through a shallow fishpond.

"Whoa," Jake grunted as they bounced over stone planters and mangled statuary.

Cecilia felt as if she was going to throw up. "Do you see him?"

"I can't see anything with these bushes stuck to the windshield."

She wrestled with the steering wheel as the Cayenne plowed through a grove of young mountain laurel bushes and up over the crest of the hill, catching a front wheel on the top step of the garden.

The Cayenne spun around and slid, rear end first, onto the circular drive in front of Brian's dorm.

Beverly's Maserati was already parked on the other side of the circle, and Cecilia saw a man in a shearling coat on the sidewalk near the car. He took off for the dorm door when the Cayenne screeched to a stop.

Cecilia and Jake bolted from the SUV as the man Cecilia could only assume was Gordon ran for the dorm steps.

The guy was an animated tree stump, solid and thick. The solar streetlights around the circle gave him a greenish hue.

Cecilia's lungs gave out, and Jake sped ahead, tackling Gordon before he set foot on the steps.

The two men rolled around in the grass, grunting and cursing. Cecilia could see Jake fumbling in his pocket, trying to reach the pepper spray, until Gordon got the upper hand. He straddled Jake's chest, pulling a gun out of the waistband of his pants and pointing it at Jake's face.

Cecilia bit back a scream. She reached them in seconds.

"Let him go," she said.

"Cecilia Katz, I presume."

"Please, let him go," Cecilia said. "I have what you want in the car. You don't need to do this."

"I'd like to believe you, but you'll have to excuse me if I don't take your word for it. Nigel told me you asked him to stall me. Then you send the bimbo to take care of me, but she doesn't have my stuff. Then I see the cops where you tell me to meet you. So what do you think? Should I trust you?"

"I understand your frustration, but the man you're pointing that gun at doesn't have anything to do with this. Please, don't hurt him."

Gordon jabbed Jake's cheek with the gun barrel. "Just get me my stuff, and we'll see where we are. Okay?"

"Okay."

She couldn't move. This maniac was too close to where her son lay sleeping. He had a gun on Jake. She was afraid if she moved, the scales would somehow tip and all would be lost.

"Go," Gordon said. "*Now.*"

She gave Jake a look that tried to convey everything she felt, but it was impossible. She backed away slowly, turning to run to the car only when she couldn't see Jake's eyes anymore.

She fumbled around under the front seat, where she'd stuffed the bag after they'd left the house. She couldn't get her fingers to work.

Finally, her fingertips brushed it. She grabbed the bag and jogged back across the circle.

"Stop there. Just throw it to me."

She tossed the bag to Gordon, and it landed with a *thop* beside him on the grass. "There. Now let him go."

Gordon grabbed the bag and took the gun away from Jake's face, tucking it back into his waistband. "Now that wasn't so hard, was it? You see how easy things can be when you—"

The wail of a siren echoed up from the bottom of the hill.

In a nanosecond Gordon pulled the gun again and grabbed Jake by the jacket collar, hauling him to his feet.

Cecilia started toward them, but Gordon pumped a shot into the air, walking backward toward the Maserati with Jake.

"What are you doing? Let him go!"

Cecilia glanced over her shoulder as two police cars sped up the hill toward the dorm. Gordon opened the door to the Maserati and tried to shove Jake inside.

Jake struggled and finally managed to get the can of

pepper spray out of his pocket. He reached up and blasted Gordon in the face.

Gordon yelped, clawing at his eyes. His gun discharged, and Jake fell to the ground, clutching his leg.

Cecilia screamed. She rushed the men, launching herself at Gordon's knees. The fumes of the pepper spray constricted her throat. She fought to breathe.

She knocked Gordon to the ground, grabbing one of his wrists and clicking the handcuff around it. He yanked his other arm away before she could complete the job, waving the gun wildly over his head.

And then Quincy was there, roused from his nap by her screams and hypnotized by the shiny flash of gunmetal in the light of the streetlamp.

He dove at the weapon, knocking it onto the asphalt.

It skittered under the Maserati, and Quincy went after it, wedging his giant head under the low-slung body of the car, pawing and whining.

The sirens sounded from halfway up the hill, and Cecilia's last thought before Gordon threw her off him was that she only had to keep him down for one more minute.

She popped up in the air and landed with a thud on the pavement, the air knocked out of her lungs. Gordon straggled to his knees, diving under the car, searching for the gun with unseeing eyes.

Quincy came up with it in his mouth, dancing in circles as if he'd just won a game of Bobbing for Handguns.

"Quincy, do *not* eat that gun!" Cecilia shouted. "Come here! Come!"

Quincy hesitated, but by some miracle ran toward her. She snagged the gun from his mouth as he ran by, rolling to her feet and heading toward Gordon.

Gordon scrambled over the hood of the Maserati and climbed into the driver's seat. Cecilia made it to the car in time to see him trying to get the key in the ignition.

She pounded on the passenger's side window, but when he fired up the engine, she knew she had to do something to stop him.

Without thinking, Cecilia pressed the barrel of the gun against the window, closed her eyes, and squeezed the trigger.

The glass shattered.

Gordon slumped over the steering wheel even as his foot hit the gas pedal. The car lurched forward.

Cecilia dove through the space that used to be the window, straining to reach the keys as the car bounced over the curb and onto the grass. She hooked a finger in the key ring and pulled. The car engine died, and the car glided to a stop just before it hit the stone steps.

Through the windshield of the car, Cecilia could see a pajama-clad Victor Newhouse peering out of the glass door, awash in the blue flashing lights of the police vehicles that now flooded the parking circle.

Gordon lay slumped over the steering wheel, unmoving.

By the time Cecilia extracted herself from the car window, there was an officer running toward her, gun drawn. Cecilia put up her hands and collapsed onto the sidewalk.

TEN MINUTES LATER, the ambulances arrived.

Cecilia had given the police a quick rundown on what had happened at the school, including a description of Beverly, which they immediately sent out over the radio. Cecilia said a quick but heartfelt prayer for her.

Gordon was still unconscious but expected to live. Jake had been shot in the leg. The bullet shattered his kneecap.

Cecilia walked beside the gurney as they wheeled him to the ambulance. Across the field, the bells of St. Anthony's pealed.

"Midnight," Jake said, his voice hoarse.

"Yes," she said. "Is it too late to make my confession?"

Jake smiled. "You better hurry."

She took his hand, gently winding her fingers through his. "Jake Eamon, you were absolutely right. I want you and I need you and I hope that we can see where this will lead."

"And?"

She took a breath. "And I pledge my undying love."

A burly cop elbowed her out of the way. "Touching, but aren't you a little old for him?"

She watched the ambulance drive away, then called to Quincy, who was sniffing around the wrecked Maserati.

He wouldn't come. What a surprise.

Cecilia walked toward the car. "Quincy, come. Come on, boy."

The dog sat stubbornly beside the car, his tail thumping loudly. Or, wait. *Was* that his tail?

She moved closer and heard the sound again. Louder this time.

Thump-thump-bump. Thump-bump.

Quincy whined and sniffed at the trunk.

Uh-oh.

Cecilia waved a cop over, and he popped open the trunk. Beverly emerged from the depths like a creature rising from the swamp, rumpled and muddy, her face streaked with mascara, her hair a tangled mess.

"Beverly. Oh, thank God. You're alive." Cecilia tried to help her out.

Beverly smacked Cecilia's hands away. "As if you care."

Obviously, her time in the trunk hadn't led to any epiphanies.

Beverly slithered out of the Maserati and attempted to smooth the wrinkles from her skirt. As if that was her biggest problem.

"Nice friends you've got," she hissed.

Cecilia shrugged. "Hey, I warned you not to steal my clients."

"You're a psychopath."

"You're a mess."

Beverly hooked the arm of the cop who opened the trunk and pulled him over to Cecilia. "Officer, you've got to arrest this woman. She's a cocaine dealer."

Cecilia sighed. It was going to be a long night.

She had absolutely no idea what might happen to her. Surprisingly, though, she felt more at peace than she had in months.

Beverly may not have had any epiphanies, but Cecilia had a few.

She didn't want to be a cobra with tits.

She realized she didn't like herself all that much, and hadn't for a long time. Once, she could have imagined nothing better than to be like Monty Frye—driven, consumed, successful. Living and breathing real estate. But where was Monty now?

Taking the big dirt nap at a mere fifty-nine years old.

While he'd lived, he'd spent more time with clients than his own family, missing his son's graduation to make settlement on a nine-bedroom contemporary, cutting out of his daughter's wedding to show a condo.

Cecilia didn't know what she wanted anymore, but she didn't want that.

She looked up at the darkened dorm and could have sworn she saw Brian's face peering out of his window. She smiled and waved, just in case.

"Come on, Quince," she said. "Let's go face the music."

CHAPTER 28

"Kid," said Cecilia to her new partner Jake, a lollipop stick dangling between her teeth—it was a permanent accessory now that she'd quit smoking—"the best piece of advice I can give you is this—real estate isn't everything."

The bells of St. Anthony's pealed noon as Cecilia got out of her new used Honda in front of the Catalina School.

Although Brian no longer attended the school—he now lived at home with her—she had a meeting with Melvin Weber about paying reparations for the garden she'd destroyed.

But there was something else she had to do first.

She walked across the field next to the boys' dorm to St. Anthony's, removing her sunglasses as she stepped into the hushed darkness of the church.

In the sanctuary, the air was thick with the scent of candle wax and incense. A few people sat quietly in the pews beside the confessionals, waiting to purge their sins.

Cecilia made the sign of the cross and slid onto a pew, closing her eyes as she examined her conscience and said the

Act of Contrition. When it was her turn, she stepped into the confessional, and it was as if she were stepping back in time.

She inhaled the scent of sin and Lemon Pledge, and all the Saturday afternoons of her youth flooded back to her....

Bless me, Father, for I have sinned. I put a tack in my brother's shoe...a toad in my teacher's desk drawer...hair remover in Mary Beth Zigler's shampoo bottle... A fifth of vodka in the punch at the sorority mixer...

She couldn't decide if it was good to be back. But she had promised God she'd come, and here she was.

She kneeled on the velvet-covered kneeler and folded her hands on the ledge. The priest slid open the divider with a *shhht*.

Through the screen, she could make out a white cassock, an abundance of gray hair and heavy jowls.

"Yes, my child?" The priest's voice was low and comforting.

"Bless me, Father, for I have sinned. It's been twelve years since my last confession."

"Go on, please."

"Well, let's see. I swore roughly 22,000 times, took the Lord's name in vain about 7,000 times, and used birth control 3,500 times."

"I see. Is that all?"

"Not even close, I'm afraid. But for the sake of brevity, I'm going to limit the big stuff to the last few weeks. Okay with you, Father?"

The priest cleared his throat, which Cecilia took as a yes.

"Here goes." She took a deep breath. "I hosted two gigolo parties, transported illegal drugs, had relations with a man who isn't my husband, broke into a car lot, lied to a police officer, destroyed a garden and shot a man."

The silence was long, and had begun to get uncomfortable when the priest finally said, "My dear. You certainly have been busy."

"Yes, Father."

"Do you take responsibility for your sins, and are you sorry for them?"

"Yes, Father." Well, most of them, anyway.

"Then for your penance, say twenty Our Fathers and twenty Hail Marys. And please, don't be a stranger. I sense you are in desperate need of guidance."

"You may be right," Cecilia said, slipping her sunglasses on. "But if there's one thing I've learned in all this, it's that sometimes you've just got to say what the heck."

She walked out of the church into the bright November sunlight, feeling like a new woman.

She'd certainly gotten good at that in the last couple of weeks.

She'd quit Belkin-Frye to start her own agency. So far Marjorie and Devon were her only clients, but she and Jake were having a blast working from her kitchen while he recovered.

She'd started divorce proceedings, and had forgiven Ben

for being such a slimeball. She figured he just couldn't help it, what with the mother he'd been cursed with.

And she'd learned to ignore the stares and elbow-jabbing from others that always seemed to accompany her outings with Jake. Hey, it took her long enough to accept their relationship. It was going to take a small miracle to get the rest of the world to understand.

Whatever was in store for her in the future, she could handle it. She had Brian and Jake and a clear conscience—at least for the moment.

She also had no office, no money and absolutely no idea how she was going to pay the Catalina School, her lawyers, her mortgage and her bills.

But she had a feeling she'd think of something.

Turn the page for an exciting sneak preview from
SUMMER DREAMS,
available in July 2007 from NEXT.

Jane Whitcomb was happy. She had to be happy.

So why in the sam hill was there salty moisture jammed up under her closed eyes?

When she got to that damned Caribbean island, Jane told herself, she was going to kick herself but good. And that old summer song about Kokomo suddenly strolled into her mind again. Soothing her. Easing away all that stress from her job as an attorney. It had been three years since her divorce...and three years since her last vacation. She closed her eyes.

It was a minute later...no more. She positively hadn't slept a wink. Not a single one.

Yet she was suddenly startled to hear a young girl's voice rise in a scream of fear.

Instead of bright morning light pouring in the port

windows of the jet, it was darker than pitch outside…and the plane seemed to be pitching, as well. Another female voice cried out.

The pilot's voice came on the loudspeaker, his tone calm but terse. "I know the turbulence is unpleasant, but please stay calm. As soon as we're on the ground, as fast as we can exit you all from the plane, we'll be aiming straight for a protected area. I understand that you'll be concerned about your luggage and your plans, but there will be no flights out of the Kokomo area until these storms have passed. We can't outrun these storms, folks, so just stay calm, and we'll be on the ground as fast as we can get you there."

Jane heard him, but her attention was abruptly ransomed by the view outside her window. From a thick clot of smoky-black clouds, a funnel suddenly shot downward. Then a second funnel. When the jet turned to approach the runway, a passenger on the other side of the aisle shrieked, "Tornadoes! We're all going to die! Can you see the tornadoes?"

But then another voice intervened. A man's voice, saying, "It's going to be all right. We'll be on the ground in less than a minute now. We're all going to be fine."

That voice…it was crazy, but Jane knew that voice.

Danger electrified the air in the cabin. It was hard to make sense of anything in the next few minutes—the crazy darkness. What time it was. Where they were. The storms had shown up from a crystal-clear sky as if from nowhere. The jet bounced on the tarmac, the brakes screeching no louder than everyone's heartbeats. Jane could taste fear at the back of her throat. Not the kind of fear she associated with stress and pressure, but the other kind. The *real* kind.

Yet that man's voice kept echoing in her mind, butter-coating her nerves, soothing her. She just…believed that voice. Believed what he said about being fine. Some instinct kept reassuring her that she knew the voice, knew the man speaking, knew she could trust him.

The elderly man across the aisle suddenly looked right at her. "Where *are* we, do you know?" Jane asked.

"Kokomo," he responded. "And it seems like we're going to make it there by the skin of our teeth."

But when Jane looked out, past the black clouds and the tumultuous wind and deluge of a rain…she saw no sign of a tropical paradise. The view revealed a flat landscape, backdropped by the buildings of a middle-size ordinary American town, with farm country visible in the far distance.

Naturally if they needed to make an emergency landing, it didn't matter where they were. But she was confused by the other passenger's response.

"This can't be Kokomo," she said.

The man raised one shaggy white eyebrow. "I promise you, it is. I was born in Kokomo, Indiana. I should know."

Kokomo, *Indiana?* Her assistant had sent her to the

wrong place! Jane stared at the man in complete bewild-
erment—but a second later, the jet slammed to a stop and
the passengers hustled toward the doors in a fury of frantic
pandemonium.

Romantic
SUSPENSE

Sparked by Danger, Fueled by Passion.

Mission: Impassioned

A brand-new miniseries begins with

My Spy

By *USA TODAY* bestselling author

Marie Ferrarella

She had to trust him with her life....
It was the most daring mission of Joshua Lazlo's
career: rescuing the prime minister of England's
daughter from a gang of cold-blooded kidnappers.
But nothing prepared the shadowy secret agent
for a fiery woman whose touch ignited something
far more dangerous.

My Spy

#1472

Available July 2007 wherever you buy books!

REQUEST YOUR
FREE BOOKS!

2 FREE NOVELS
PLUS 2
FREE GIFTS!

There's the life you planned. And there's what comes next.

YES! Please send me 2 FREE Harlequin® NEXT™ novels and my 2 FREE mystery gifts. After receiving them, if I don't wish to receive any more books, I can return the shipping statement marked "cancel." If I don't cancel, I will receive 4 brand-new novels every other month and be billed just $3.99 per book in the U.S. or $4.74 per book in Canada, plus 25¢ shipping and handling per book plus applicable taxes, if any.* That's a savings of over 25% off the cover price! I understand that accepting the 2 free books and gifts places me under no obligation to buy anything. I can always return a shipment and cancel at any time. Even if I never buy anything from Harlequin, the two free books and gifts are mine to keep forever. .   155 HDN EL33   355 HDN EL4F

Name   (PLEASE PRINT)

Address   Apt. #

City   State/Prov.   Zip/Postal Code

Signature (if under 18, a parent or guardian must sign)

Order online at www.TryNEXTNovels.com
Or mail to the **Harlequin Reader Service®**:
IN U.S.A.: P.O. Box 1867, Buffalo, NY 14240-1867
IN CANADA: P.O. Box 609, Fort Erie, Ontario L2A 5X3

Not valid to current Harlequin NEXT subscribers.
Want to try two free books from another line?
Call 1-800-873-8635 or visit www.morefreebooks.com

* Terms and prices subject to change without notice. NY residents add applicable sales tax. Canadian residents will be charged applicable provincial taxes and GST. This offer is limited to one order per household. All orders subject to approval. Credit or debit balances in a customer's account(s) may be offset by any other outstanding balance owed by or to the customer. Please allow 4 to 6 weeks for delivery.

Your Privacy: Harlequin Books is committed to protecting your privacy. Our Privacy Policy is available online at www.eHarlequin.com or upon request from the Harlequin Reader Service. From time to time we make our lists of customers available to reputable firms who may have a product or service of interest to you. If you would prefer we not share your name and address, please check here. ☐

NEXT07R

Always passionate, always proud.

**The richest royal family in the world—
a family united by blood and passion,
torn apart by deceit and desire.**

Step into the glamorous, enticing world of the
Nirolian Royal Family. As the king ails he must find an
heir…each month an exciting new installment follows
the epic search for the true Nirolian king. Eight heirs,
eight romances, eight fantastic stories!

It's time for playboy prince Marco Fierezza to
claim his rightful place…on the throne of Niroli!
Emily loves Marco, but she has no idea he's a royal
prince! What will this king-in-waiting do when he
discovers his mistress is pregnant?

THE FUTURE KING'S PREGNANT MISTRESS

by Penny Jordan

(#2643)

On sale July 2007.

HP12643

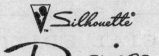

THE GARRISONS

A brand-new family saga begins with

THE CEO'S
SCANDALOUS AFFAIR
BY ROXANNE ST. CLAIRE

Eldest son Parker Garrison is preoccupied running
his Miami hotel empire and dealing with his recently
deceased father's secret second family. Since he has
little time to date, taking his superefficient assistant
to a charity event should have been a simple plan.
Until passion takes them beyond business.

Don't miss any of the six exciting titles in
THE GARRISONS continuity, beginning in July.
Only from Silhouette Desire.

THE CEO'S
SCANDALOUS AFFAIR
#1807

Available July 2007.

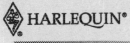 **HARLEQUIN®**

COMING NEXT MONTH

#87 STORM SEASON • Charlotte Douglas

It's hurricane season, and Pelican Bay P.I. Maggie Skerritt and her partner Bill Malcolm are facing a perfect storm of their own. A syndicated columnist stalked by a sniper, a stranger with amnesia, even Bill's ex-wife have all hit town. There's a category-five mystery brewing…and the answers are blowing in the hundred-mile-an-hour wind.

#88 SUMMER DREAMS • Kate Austin, Jennifer Greene and Stevi Mittman

Here are three must-read stories about raising families, solving mysteries, climbing the career ladder and rediscovering long-lost loves under the sizzling summer sun. The bottom line—life's a beach, and these irrepressible women are loving every minute of it!

NXTCNM0607